She stood perfectly still in the doorway. His appearance took her breath away, and she stared at him in shock for a moment, not quite able to take in this vision of perfect masculinity.

He was long and lean and dressed in immaculate dark trousers and a pristine shirt in a shade of blue that matched his eyes. He looked every inch the consultant—alert, energetic, commanding respect.

He was heart-meltingly attractive.

She was disturbed by the way he managed to upset her peace of mind. Wasn't he the source of a lot of her troubles? Why was she so aware of a man who could distance himself from love and family feeling and keep himself detached from a good part of what made for normal human emotions?

She needed to keep up her guard, and not allow herself to fall for him. He was simply her boss...who also happened to be the bothersome man living next door.

There was no escaping him.

When **Joanna Neil** discovered Mills & Boon®, her life-long addiction to reading crystallised into an exciting new career writing Medical™ Romance. Her characters are probably the outcome of her varied lifestyle, which includes working as a clerk, typist, nurse and infant teacher. She enjoys dressmaking and cooking at her Leicestershire home. Her family includes a husband, son and daughter, an exuberant yellow Labrador and two slightly crazed cockatiels. She currently works with a team of tutors at her local education centre, to provide creative writing workshops for people interested in exploring their own writing ambitions.

Recent titles by the same author:

THE LONDON CONSULTANT'S RESCUE
THE EMERGENCY DOCTOR'S PROPOSAL
HER BOSS AND PROTECTOR
THE LONDON DOCTOR

EMERGENCY AT RIVERSIDE HOSPITAL

BY
JOANNA NEIL

MILLS & BOON®
Pure reading pleasure

First published in Great Britain 2007
Large Print edition 2007
Harlequin Mills & Boon Limited,
Eton House, 18-24 Paradise Road.
Richmond, Surrey TW9 1SR

© Joanna Neil 2007

ISBN: 978 0 263 19548 4

Set in Times Roman 16¾ on 19 pt.
17-1107-54136

Printed and bound in Great Britain
by Antony Rowe Ltd, Chippenham, Wiltshire

Neil, Joanna

Emergency at
Riverside
Hospital /
                    LP

1789814

EMERGENCY AT RIVERSIDE HOSPITAL

CHAPTER ONE

IT WAS an odd feeling, coming back to the house where she had lived for all of her childhood. The memories were a mixture of happiness and sadness, and Kayleigh couldn't be sure which one outweighed the other. She hesitated, looking up at the whitewashed walls, splashed with colour from hanging baskets that spilled over with the bright, delicate blooms of fuchsias and petunias. The flowers, at least, gladdened her heart.

The house was built on an incline, fronting onto a cobbled street that meandered down towards a small cove. This part of the North Devon coastline was beautiful, and the house overlooked the sea, albeit from a distance.

After a moment's hesitation, Kayleigh started up the raised access towards the front door, fingering the black wrought-iron balustrade that edged the walkway. The air was fresh and clean, with a hint of sea spray in the air, and she breathed it in, filling her lungs.

The walk up here from the harbour had been invigorating, but now she frowned a little, thinking about it. How was Aunt Jane coping with the difficult gradient and the cobbled pathways these days? She wasn't getting any younger, was she?

Kayleigh turned her key in the lock and let herself into the house. Perhaps this strange, hollow sensation in her stomach was there because she knew that her mother was no longer around to greet her. A wave of sadness washed over her, but she braced herself, straightening her shoulders, and wandered through to the kitchen and then the sitting room in search of her aunt.

A rustling sound was coming from the study, and she almost turned to go there, but then she saw that the patio doors were open to let in the warmth of the sunshine, and instead she went to glance out over the garden. Her spirits lifted when she saw that her aunt was there, sitting out on the terrace.

'So this is where you're hiding…' Kayleigh said with a smile, going outside to greet her.

Aunt Jane's face lit up, her mouth curving with pleasure. 'Kayleigh, love…you're here…I was wondering if you would make it after all— I know how busy you are these days with your job at the hospital. It's so good to see you.' She made to get up, but Kayleigh waved her back down into her seat.

'You stay where you are,' she said hurriedly. 'I'll come and join you.' She hadn't missed the tired lines that had etched the older woman's face before she had realised that her niece was here, and there had been a faint droop to her shoulders, too. A swift surge of concern flooded through Kayleigh. It was something of a shock to see her aunt looking this way.

How long had it been since she had last seen her…five or six months?…and yet the change in her was so noticeable. Aunt Jane had always been sprightly, forever busy doing this and that. It seemed age was finally beginning to creep up on her.

'Are you feeling all right?' Kayleigh asked in a tentative fashion. Her aunt's brown hair was faded and streaked with grey, framing her face with soft waves that emphasised her careworn features. 'You're looking quite pale.'

'Oh, I'm fine. Don't you go worrying about me. You can put your doctor's hat away.' Aunt Jane brushed the sympathy to one side with her usual forthrightness, putting on a cheerful face. 'I'm just a little weary, that's all. I thought I would come out here for a breath of air, and give myself a few minutes to gather my thoughts... It's very peaceful out here.' She gave a faint sigh. 'Though, looking at the garden, I can see lots of things that need doing.'

Kayleigh followed her aunt's glance. Beyond the terrace where they were sitting, there was a wide expanse of lawn, edged with generous, curving herbaceous borders. The shrubs added a riot of vibrant colour, but they tumbled over with exuberant life and threatened to swamp one another in their efforts to fill every inch of available space. The fruit trees promised an abundant crop later in the season, and at the far end of the garden the shed was almost hidden from view by a crab-apple tree whose branches were weighed down with blossom. The lawn, though, had been neatly trimmed.

Her brow furrowed. 'I'll try to do something about it over the next week or so, now that I'm here.'

Her eyes narrowed as she caught sight of a shadowy figure that seemed to flit behind the crab-apple tree, but then it was gone and she decided she must have been imagining things. She shook her head. Perhaps she was more uptight than she had realised.

'I know I ought to have come to help out before this,' she murmured, 'but there has been so much to do, with getting used to different shift patterns and taking my specialist exams, and so on.'

'I know, love.' Aunt Jane reached out and patted her hand. 'But it's working out well for you, isn't it? You've always hankered after being an A and E doctor, haven't you?'

Kayleigh nodded. 'For as far back as I can remember.' She was thoughtful. 'I think it was after my dad died that I knew I had to go into medicine. I wanted to do what I could to help people, to learn how to save lives.'

Aunt Jane's mouth lifted at the corners. 'I knew that you would do all right for yourself. I said as much to your mother.' She was silent for a moment, and then added, 'Of course, I guessed some time ago that it would be too much for you to keep on this old house and go on working out of town…and there's that boyfriend of yours, too. I know you have a lot going on.'

'There's no boyfriend…not any longer.' Kayleigh made a face. 'It didn't work out.'

'It didn't?'

'No. He seemed perfect to begin with, but later on I realised that he was way too controlling, wanting everything his own way. Besides, I caught him in a clinch with one of the nurses when I changed my shift pattern and went home early one day, and that was the final straw. He's history.'

'Oh, dear.' Aunt Jane looked upset. 'I'm so sorry. You deserve better.'

Kayleigh's mouth made an odd shape. 'I'm all right…but I am sorry that I've left you here for so long on your own. I know this house is too much for you. I really wanted to come back and see you before this.'

'I can imagine how difficult things have been for you. As to this place, it's a grand house, but it was one thing looking after it when your mother was alive, but now…well, I'm not as fit as I used to be, and it's such a big, rambling place, more than I can handle, I have to admit. It needs a lot of love and care to keep it the way it should be.' She sent Kayleigh a direct look. 'Have you decided what you're going to do about it?'

Kayleigh shook her head. 'I haven't made up my mind yet.' She pulled a face. 'I suppose I've been putting it off.'

Her aunt nodded. 'I imagine, now that probate has come through, the best thing will be for you to put it on the market and tie up all the loose ends.'

'We'll see. I know I need to get to grips with it, and it's something we definitely need to talk about.' Kayleigh was distracted, her attention caught by a flash of movement glimpsed through the study window. She frowned. 'Is there someone in the house? I thought I heard a noise coming from the study when I first arrived.'

Aunt Jane made a face. 'That'll be your step-father. He came just a while ago. I tried to send him packing, but he was in a bit of a strop, and he pushed on straight past me. He seems to think he'll find some share certificates tucked away in a drawer somewhere…though why he's decided to come after them now, I don't know. Maybe it's because time's running out and his options are dwindling.'

Kayleigh stiffened. 'Whatever the reason—he can't just come barging in here whenever he likes.'

'No. Well, I thought maybe I would leave him to it for a while and let him get things out of his system. I figured that when he didn't find anything he would eventually up and leave.' She pondered that for a second or two and then gave a faint nod, as though she had come to some sort of internal conclusion. 'Perhaps he's been in there long enough.' She started to get slowly to her feet, and Kayleigh could see that the action was an effort for her and that her joints must be complaining.

'No, no…I'll go and deal with him,' Kayleigh said. 'Leave him to me.' But just as she was about to march towards the house to go and sort things out, she was jolted by a clatter that seemed to come from the other end of the garden, from inside the garden shed. She stopped, and peered through the veil of greenery. 'Is there someone in the shed as well?'

'I don't think so, dear.' Her aunt looked back at the house and appeared flustered. 'Maybe the cat came in from down the road and knocked something over. He does that sometimes.'

Aunt Jane seemed vague about what might be going on, and Kayleigh couldn't see a window open where a cat might have got in. There was a break in the fence, though, big enough to let in an intruder. She started across the lawn to investigate. Her stepfather could wait for the moment.

As she drew closer to the shed, a voice said, 'Ah, there you are. Found you at last.' There was no one to be seen, but Kayleigh realised that it was a man's voice that she was hearing...not one that she recognised, and those certainly weren't her stepfather's usual harsh tones. This was more a husky male drawl of satisfaction.

A second or two later, the man appeared, framed in the doorway of the shed. He was so tall that he had to stoop a little to avoid the lintel, and as he straightened up, Kayleigh was taken aback by the sudden vision of powerful masculinity, strong legs encased in denim, rippling biceps emphasised by the T-shirt he was wearing. His hair was jet black, stylishly cut to frame his angular face.

He was holding two large cans of paint by the straps, one in either hand, and he glanced at both in turn before looking across at Kayleigh. Seeing her, he stopped in his tracks, and for a moment his eyes widened and his head went back, as though he was stunned by what he saw. Perhaps he hadn't expected to come across anyone down there.

He recovered soon enough from whatever it was that had thrown him, and looked her up and down, his gaze drifting over the shapely feminine curves outlined by the cotton top she was wearing, and it was clear from his glinting expression that he had taken on board the way the filmy fabric of her skirt casually draped itself around the long line of her legs. His blue gaze came to rest on her long hair, lingering momentarily on the bright chestnut curls that danced with light under the warm rays of the sun.

'Hello, there,' he said, on a faintly guarded note. He inclined his head a fraction in greeting. 'Which do you think, magnolia or buttermilk?' His voice was a low rumble of dark chocolate that wrapped itself enticingly around her senses.

'I beg your pardon?' Kayleigh stared at him.

'I can't make up my mind which one to use.' He shrugged. 'I have a few interior walls that I need to paint.'

Kayleigh drew in a deep breath. What was this man doing here, rummaging through the shed as though he had every right to be on this property? Had he simply decided to brazen things out because he had been caught in the act of helping himself? Was her aunt surrounded by people who were ready to take advantage of her? Clearly, she had stayed away from here for far too long, and things were beginning to get out of hand.

'I don't think I can help you with that,' she said, her tone edged with suspicion. 'I'm not at all sure who you are and why you're here.'

'Likewise,' he said, and he actually looked at her as though she were the interloper. 'I don't believe I've seen you around here before today.' He looked at her questioningly. He didn't seem to be at all put out by her watchful manner, and she felt a slight resentment bubbling up inside her that he should be questioning her entitlement to be here.

She turned to see if her aunt could throw some light on the matter, but Aunt Jane must have gone inside the house, because she was nowhere to be seen. Instead, Kayleigh's stepfather came storming out into the garden, looking like a thundercloud that was about to burst. He was heading towards her, his body taut, his over-long black hair unkempt, as though he had been raking his hands through it.

'So you've come back, have you?' he bit out, glaring at her. 'I suppose you think you're going to waltz in here, sell up and move on?' His eyes narrowed. 'I wouldn't bank on that, if I were you.'

His sudden appearance put Kayleigh on edge, but she made up her mind to stay calm. It was bad enough him being there at all, without having a stranger standing by to witness their confrontation. Though perhaps the stranger would take advantage of the situation and disappear. 'Why is that, Evan?'

'Because I have rights, too. Don't think you can get away with this.'

She looked him straight in the eyes. 'I've no idea what you think I'm getting away with. I do know that you can't simply walk in here whenever you feel like it. You don't live here any more.' She said that last bit with slow, clear emphasis.

He moved closer to her, his face a few centimetres away from hers, his whole manner aggressive, threatening her with his sheer bulk. 'Don't you talk to me that way, girl. I'm your father and you'll take note of what I say.'

Kayleigh shook her head. 'No way are you my father…and don't think for one second that you can browbeat me the way you did my sister.'

His face contorted. 'I was married to your mother, and that puts me in charge, do you hear? This house should be mine, and I left papers here, certificates and documents, things that belong to me. I know they were in the bureau, but now they've gone. That must have been your doing. You had no right to take them.' He spat the words out, his lips tight with anger.

'I don't have them. Anything of any relevance is in the hands of the solicitor, so perhaps you should go and talk to him about anything you think belongs to you. As to the house, as far as I'm concerned, all that was sorted in your divorce settlement.'

'Your mother died before that went through.' His tone was sneering.

'Maybe…but she had time to put all her affairs in order and she made sure that I knew what was to be done. I guess you didn't know about the will until it was too late.'

An expression of rage crossed his face. 'You put her up to it, didn't you?' He made to lunge at her, and Kayleigh made a quick step backwards to avoid him, only to find that the assault didn't carry through. She blinked, wondering why that was. Then she saw that the stranger had abandoned his paint cans and had hold of Evan's arm in a vice-like grip. Her stepfather was suddenly rendered impotent.

'I don't think you want to go there,' her rescuer said softly, his focus purely on Evan. His body was poised for action, perfectly fit and honed, and it was abundantly clear who was the stronger man.

Kayleigh stared at him. As she was floundering, coming to terms with the fact that he had bothered to stay around, her aunt appeared, brandishing a broom.

'It's time you were going,' Aunt Jane said,

glowering at Evan. She angled the broom towards him. 'I hope you weren't thinking of giving us an argument about it.'

Perhaps Evan would have contemplated doing that if he had been faced with just the two women he had expected to encounter, but the tall stranger seemed to have the advantage of him. Evan wasn't about to push his luck, not until he knew more about his opposition.

'I've said what I came to say,' he muttered. He sent a fulminating glance in the direction of Kayleigh and Aunt Jane. 'You haven't heard the last of this. I'll see you two in court.'

He tried to wrench his arm from the manacle that held him fast and, seeing that he was turning away, the man let him go. Kayleigh followed her stepfather through the house and watched him leave, making sure that she saw his car drive away before she went back to the garden.

She expected that her aunt might still be down by the shed, but when she came back through the patio doors she was concerned to see that the older woman was unwell, in a state of near collapse. The man was helping her back towards the terrace, his arm about her waist.

'Aunt Jane…' Kayleigh hurried towards them. 'Let's settle her down on to the sun lounger,' she told the man. 'I can adjust the backrest for her.'

She sent her aunt a worried look. 'What is it? What's wrong? Has this happened before?'

'Just a little…breathless…' her aunt managed. 'Be all right…in a minute…'

'She was dizzy and almost fainted,' the man said. He was checking the pulse at her wrist as he spoke. 'Her heart's racing. I suspect the set-to with your stepfather has been too much for her.'

'Has this happened before?' Kayleigh was speaking to her aunt, but the man answered for her.

'Yes, a couple of times. She's been exhausted lately. I've tried to tell her that she needs to see someone about it and get herself checked out.'

Kayleigh glanced at him. 'So you and my aunt know each other?'

He nodded. 'I'm living in the house next door— or rather I'm looking after the property while the owner's away. Your aunt and I have come to know each other quite well over the last few weeks.'

Kayleigh frowned. 'Oh, I see.' That still didn't explain why he had been poking around in the shed, but she supposed that explanation could wait. There were other priorities to be dealt with right now.

She gently stroked her aunt's shoulder. 'I want to go and get my medical bag from the house,' she said. 'Do you think you'll be all right for a minute or two if I leave you?'

Aunt Jane nodded, but didn't say anything, and Kayleigh guessed that her condition was worsening. She looked up at the man. 'Will you stay with her?'

'Yes, of course.'

She was back within a couple of minutes, and she swiftly knelt down beside her aunt, wrapping a blood-pressure cuff around her arm.

'I just want to see how you're doing,' she said. Then, after a moment or two, she muttered, 'That's way too high, and your pulse is erratic.' She held her aunt's hand and looked at her in concern. 'Aunt Jane, I think we need to get you to hospital for an ECG, so that we can see what's going on with your heart.'

'No, no…I don't want that…' Her aunt looked at the man for help. Her eyes were desperate. 'Lewis, tell her…'

He shook his head sadly. 'She's right, though, Jane.' Lewis hunkered down beside her. 'Your pulse is too fast, and your blood pressure needs to be brought down. We have to find out what's wrong.'

Aunt Jane shook her head. 'No hospital,' she said, her voice frail. 'I don't want to go to hospital.' She paused to get her breath and looked pleadingly at Kayleigh. 'You can give me something that will help...can't you?'

Kayleigh hesitated. The doctor's surgery would be closed for the weekend, and if her aunt wouldn't go to hospital there were few options left. 'Only if you promise that you'll see your GP on Monday.'

Aunt Jane nodded and closed her eyes briefly.

'What are you going to do?' Lewis asked, his blue gaze shifting to Kayleigh.

'I'll give her a calcium channel blocker, to see if that will help settle things down. If that doesn't work, I'll have to have a rethink. She may still have to go to hospital.'

'She ought to be on oxygen in the meantime. Her breathing's not right. I'll see to that while you sort out the medication.'

She glanced at him, her eyes narrowing. 'Have I missed something? You seem to know all about what's going on...are you a doctor?'

He nodded. Already he was delving into her medical kit and sorting out what he needed. 'I started work at the Riverside Hospital a few weeks ago. That's why I moved down here. I was brought in to sort out the A and E depart-ment...it was either that or suffer closures because the service is overloaded.'

Kayleigh looked at him in dismay. 'That's where I'm going to be working.' Aunt Jane's eyes fluttered open. She looked startled, staring at Kayleigh, and then she tried to speak.

'No, stay still,' Kayleigh said, laying a gentle hand on her. 'I meant to tell you about the job, but I didn't want to get your hopes up. I wasn't sure it was going to happen until the last minute. Apparently a doctor decided to leave the area, and I was offered the chance to step in and take his place.'

Her aunt looked as though she was relieved to hear the news, but she was clearly too ill to vol-unteer an opinion just then. Kayleigh gave her the medication, filling a glass tumbler with juice from an ice jug on the table and holding the glass to her aunt's lips.

'This should help,' she told her aunt, waiting while she sipped the cool liquid. 'The coldness might help to slow your heart rate a little. The tablets will take a few minutes to work, but we'll give you some oxygen to ease your breathing and make you feel more comfortable in the mean-time.'

Lewis had the equipment ready, and slipped the breathing mask into place over her face.

'Jane told me that you were working in A and E,' he murmured, glancing across at Kayleigh. 'If you're moving to Riverside, I imagine that means we could be working alongside one another.'

Kayleigh tried to absorb that. 'It looks that way, doesn't it?' She wasn't sure how she felt, learning that she would be working with this man, especially considering that hadn't got off to a very good start.

The same thought must have occurred to him. 'I wasn't making off with the paint,' he murmured. 'Your aunt said I could help myself. I just hadn't got around to it until this afternoon. I'm doing a bit of decorating while my friend is away, by way of thanking him for helping me out.'

'Oh, I see.' She didn't, though, not really.

'I was going to buy some,' he said, as though he sensed her confusion, 'but Jane said not to bother. She said you wouldn't be using up the emulsion any time soon and it would be going to waste.'

Kayleigh nodded. 'That's probably true. My mother had the walls hung with expensive paper. I don't think we'll be changing that any time soon.' She ran her tongue lightly over her lower lip. 'I should thank you for intervening back there with my stepfather...although I'm sure I would have been able to handle him on my own. He can be overbearing at times, but he's never stepped over the mark before.'

His mouth made a wry slant. 'There's always a first time, and he looked as though he was pretty close to losing it. I wasn't prepared to take the risk.'

'No, well...as I said, thank you for what you did, and thank you for helping me now, with my aunt. I hadn't realised that she was so poorly. She's always been strong, for as far back as I can remember.'

'Perhaps she's had to be. She's been coping on her own for quite a while since your mother died, from what I've gathered. You haven't been around very much at all, as far as I can see.'

She wasn't sure whether that was meant as a criticism or not. 'I've had a lot to deal with, one way and another, and the journey down here would have played havoc with my shift patterns. I did try to keep in touch by phone.'

He didn't look too impressed by that information, and something in her rebelled at having to explain herself to this virtual stranger. Who was he to sit in judgment on her?

'A phone call is an easy way to salve your conscience. It isn't quite the same as a visit, though.' His tone was cool.

'It was enough for me to be able to keep a check on how she was doing.'

He raised a dark brow. 'If you say so.' He glanced at her aunt and saw that she was sleeping. 'I think the tablets must be taking effect at last. Rest is what she needs.' He checked her aunt's pulse and then looked back at Kayleigh. 'She hasn't had much of that lately. This house is too much for her to cope with on her own, and the garden needs more than a light touch. I've helped out with cutting the lawn, and I've made a start on weeding the borders, but I know that she feels as though she's under pressure all the time. She's not well, and it's all far more than she can handle.'

'I know. I'm beginning to realise that.' She looked around, deep in thought. 'This house has always taken a lot of upkeep. My mother loved it, and it was in her family for generations, but it was different when we were all at home to share the burden. She didn't want to let it go. That's why she fought to keep Evan from getting his hands on it.'

She grimaced. 'After she died, I put every-thing in the hands of the solicitors. I just had so much to contend with, coming to terms with her passing on, trying to get my career off the ground. I still have my doubts about how I'm going to keep it all together.'

His expression was cynical. 'Evan was right, though, wasn't he? You're going to sell up and move on. Even your aunt believes that's what you'll do.'

Kayleigh's eyes widened. 'Has she confided in you?' It bothered her that this man knew more about her aunt's welfare than she did. In all the times that she had talked to Aunt Jane, the older woman had never hinted at being ill or unable to cope.

He nodded. 'We get on really well, your aunt and I. She's very fond of you, but I do know that she's afraid for the future. She knows how much your career means to you and she thinks you'll want to go on following your star.'

He looked at her steadily. 'She's not far wrong, is she? You've already admitted how important it is to you. It has certainly taken precedence over your family these last few months. Perhaps that's why your aunt is desperately afraid of becoming a burden on you. She thinks that she'll end up in a care home so that you'll be able to move on.'

Kayleigh sucked in a shocked breath. The criticism stung, and for a while she was bewildered, not knowing how to respond. How could he say these things to her?

She said tightly, 'I don't know where all this is coming from. We've only just met, and yet you seem to feel that you can pass judgment on the way I do things. You don't know the first thing about me.' She got to her feet.

'I wasn't censuring you, merely stating facts.' He stood up, coming face to face with her.

She wasn't appeased. Who was he to decide that she wasn't doing right by her aunt? He couldn't possibly know what she planned to do. She wasn't even sure of that herself.

She said curtly, 'Even so...' She braced herself. 'Thank you for helping me with my aunt, but she seems to be over the worst, at least for the time being, so I think perhaps you could leave now. Isn't there some paintwork that needs your attention?'

'That's true.' He glanced towards her aunt, who appeared to be breathing more easily, and seemed to be over the worst of her attack. 'Do you think you'll be able to manage?'

'Perfectly, thank you. As I said, I'm obliged for your help.'

'You're welcome.' His gaze narrowed on her. 'I expect we'll be seeing a lot more of each other in the weeks to come. Whatever happens, until you put up the for-sale sign, I hope your aunt knows that I'm here to help out whenever she needs me.'

She didn't answer him, but watched him walk away, taking the path through the garden and out by the break in the fence. Maybe that should be the first job on her list, organising its repair. Then the doctor next door might not feel so free to come and go as he pleased.

The thought didn't give her any pleasure. She had to acknowledge that for all his recriminations he had done a lot to help out. She ought to be thankful for that, but it was hard for her to see things his way. Inside she was wound up, as tight as a drum. All the problems she had encountered lately seemed to have been brought about because of some man or other. It left a bad taste in her mouth. She was definitely off the species.

CHAPTER TWO

'I've made an appointment for you to go and see your family doctor,' Kayleigh said, clearing the breakfast dishes from the table and stacking them in the dishwasher. She glanced at Aunt Jane, who was wiping toast crumbs from her fingers and pretending not to listen. 'He's agreed to see you when my shift finishes, so I'll be able to drive you there myself.'

That had her aunt's attention. 'It's really not necessary, dear. It was just a funny turn, that's all. I don't want him to be wasting his time— or yours, for that matter.'

'It isn't a waste of time.' Kayleigh smiled at the older woman. 'Now that I'm home, I'm going to make sure that you get the best of attention, so you need to get used to it. I'm not going to take no for an answer.'

Aunt Jane sniffed. 'You know, you can be almost as bossy as your mother was when you put your mind to it.'

Kayleigh chuckled. 'Yes, I know I can.' She slid into the seat beside her aunt and said softly, 'Seriously, though...I can see that you haven't been well, and you don't have to try to cover it up. You know I want to do what's right for you, don't you? You've been there for me all my life, and you were there for Mum when she needed you, and now it's your turn to be cosseted. Let me look after you.'

Aunt Jane's expression was troubled. 'You have enough to do, as it is. I don't want to hold you back.'

Kayleigh shook her head. 'You really mustn't think of it that way. You're my aunt, and I love you.' She hesitated. 'There are things we need to talk about, though. We need to sort out what we're going to do about this house, for a start. You said it was too big for you to cope with...does that mean that you would prefer to live in a smaller place? Should we be looking for another house—one that's more man-ageable?'

'I don't know.' Aunt Jane made a fluttery, negative movement with her hands. 'That's your decision, love. This is your house. I don't want to influence you in any way.'

Kayleigh grimaced. Wasn't that the answer she always gave? 'I wish you would help me out here. Are you really saying that you want to leave it to me? Do you trust me to do whatever I think is best?'

'Of course.' She hesitated. 'I admit I've not been well lately, and things have been getting a bit much for me. I suppose I could always find myself a place in a care home if need be, if it comes to that. I've some money put by, and your mother saw to it that I had enough to live on.'

Kayleigh patted her shoulder. 'I don't think so. That's not going to happen. You've always been strong and if you're feeling weak it's just because you're going through a bad patch right now. Don't worry about it. We'll get you back on your feet again. I promise I won't do anything without your approval—your opinion means a lot to me, you know, but we really need to get to grips with the situation soon, and make a decision of some sort.'

She got to her feet. 'For now, I just need to know that you'll come with me to see the GP after work, and that you'll take it easy for the rest of the day.'

Her aunt looked a little doubtful about that, but she gave a slight nod, all the same. 'I dare say I can do that.'

'Good.' Kayleigh frowned. 'Are you absolutely sure that you'll be all right if I go to the hospital? I could always phone in and say that I can't make it.'

'No, no…I couldn't let you do that. I've told you, I'll be fine. You go along and get yourself off to work. It's your big day, today.'

Kayleigh pulled a face. 'I don't know how I feel about bearding the lion in his den. I can't believe that I'm going to be working with that man next door. I can't imagine how we'll get on. I don't think he has too high an opinion of me.'

'Oh, but he's lovely.' Aunt Jane's expression softened. 'I'm sure that you'll get on like a house on fire.'

Kayleigh thought the analogy was probably apt. It sounded like a worrying situation that could only have a troublesome outcome, and that was most likely what she would find herself up against.

Her aunt was oblivious to any of her worries. 'I'm very fond of Lewis, you know.' Her mouth curved into a smile. 'He's been very good to me.'

'Hmm, I think that works both ways. From what I've seen over the last day or so, he's helped himself to paint, odd bits of furniture, some bed linen…'

'Only bits and pieces that I brought with me when I came here. They were no use to me, and I'm glad he found a purpose for them. I do hate to see waste.'

Kayleigh shook her head. 'I must go,' she murmured, dropping a kiss on to her aunt's forehead. 'I'm running late already and, as you say, this is my first day in the new job. I have to find my way about the place, yet.'

Some half an hour later she manoeuvred the car into a parking space and headed for the main building of the hospital. The A and E unit was situated in a block on the right-hand side and she hurried in through the glass sliding doors, searching for the consultant's office. He was holding a meeting that morning for new arrivals to the department, and with luck she would make it by the skin of her teeth.

'Dr McAllister's office is through there, second door on the right,' the receptionist told her. 'He was in early this morning—I think he may already have started the meeting. I've seen one or two people go in there, and I know he's keen to get out to A and E as soon as possible.' The girl's mouth curved. 'He's only been consultant here for a few weeks, but he's certainly managed to stir things up...the place is jumping.'

Kayleigh winced. That wasn't exactly what she wanted to hear. She was on time...just...but it sounded as though he was quick off the mark and driven, and he probably expected everyone else to be the same.

She knocked on the door of his room and went in. Lewis was standing by a whiteboard, sketching a flow chart and filling in relevant details with a black marker pen, explaining his actions as he went.

She stood perfectly still in the doorway. His appearance took her breath away, and she stared at him in shock for a moment, not quite able to take in this vision of perfect masculinity. He was wearing a beautifully tailored grey suit, his whole appearance totally different from the casually dressed man of the weekend. He looked every inch the consultant, alert, energetic, commanding respect.

'There we have it—accident scene, paramedic intervention, journey to hospital, A and E,' he said briskly, glancing at his audience. 'What happens at each stage can mean the difference between life or death for the patient.' Two young doctors, both male, looked attentive and nodded.

Lewis looked over at Kayleigh. 'So there you are, Dr Byford,' he greeted her. He raised a dark brow. 'I wasn't really expecting to see you here today.'

Kayleigh blinked. 'You weren't?' She was flustered. 'I thought this was my induction day?'

'It is.' He put down the marker pen and indicated a chair. 'Please, come in and sit down.'

She did as he asked, taking her place by the side of the two young doctors.

He said, 'I've just been talking to your colleagues about the dynamics of trauma medicine and the role of the professionals who are in attendance. In my experience it makes a huge difference to patient care if the emergency doctors understand how paramedics operate and how they come to make their assessments.'

He paused, shooting a glance over the two male house officers. 'As I was saying, each of you will have the opportunity to go out with the ambulance service at some point, but since our senior house officer has arrived, I think we'll let her have the first session. I don't need to keep either of you any longer. If you go and find the registrar, he'll look after you for the rest of the day.'

The men stood up and nodded to Kayleigh before going to speak with him quietly for a minute. Then they made their way to the door, leaving her to frown, uncertain what was expected of her.

'I'm sorry if I was late,' she began, when he had closed the door behind them. 'I thought we said eight o'clock.'

'We did. You weren't late…it's just that I wanted to make an early start. I half expected you to ring in and say that you weren't going to be able to come in today—with your aunt being ill, and all the things that go along with that.'

'She's all right. I mean, her heart rate's still all over the place, but I've given her medication and I've asked a neighbour to keep an eye on her. I've left my number in case there's a problem.' If he was going to condemn her for being heartless, she would give him a fight on that score. She wasn't uncaring, far from it...she wouldn't have dreamed of leaving Aunt Jane if she hadn't been able to make provision for her while she was at work. Her grey eyes challenged him.

'I wasn't making an issue of it,' he murmured, shrugging his shoulders in a negligent fashion. 'People have different priorities. I accept that. A good many people put their job first. They have to...it brings in an income.'

She looked at him in some confusion. Was he saying that he thought it was the norm to behave that way? That wasn't how she saw things. Clearly, he was an oddball, a maverick, and she didn't know quite what to make of him.

'Since you've come in on time, we may as well make our way to the ambulance bay,' he told her. 'We'll use the fast-response car to head out to the trauma sites.' He was already starting towards the door.

'I don't think I follow,' she said, hanging back. The whole thought of going out and about on her first day unsettled her. She had only just arrived and it wasn't at all what she had been expecting. 'I understood that the induction day meant I would be able to get to know my way around the department, get to know people, and learn what's expected of me. How can I do that if I'm not going to be staying here? Isn't it a little soon for you to be sending me out on away missions?'

He turned to stare at her, a brooding expression coming into his blue eyes. 'You might have a point there. I suppose I imagined that anyone who works in Emergency would be ready for the unexpected and be able to deal with it.' He made a grimace. 'I dare say I could rope in one of the juniors, but I thought they would benefit more from staying behind and getting used to the A and E department. Most of the other doctors on the team have specific duties today, but I imagine we could work something out.' A crooked line worked its way into his brow. 'Do you really think you won't be up to it?'

'Yes—I mean, no, I expect I'll cope…I don't think it would be a good idea to send a junior out, not at all. They have enough to deal with, getting to grips with emergency medicine.' Her grey eyes were filled with doubt. 'I'm just surprised that you want to start this project on day one. It seems an unusual course of action and, anyway, shouldn't you be overseeing the department?'

He was silent for a while, and it occurred to her that perhaps she ought not to have questioned him that way. Did he think she was undermining his authority?

'It isn't my day one.' He sent her an appraising glance. 'Actually, since you ask, I was supposed to be attending management meetings for most of the day, so I'm not actually booked in to work. The meetings were cancelled at the last minute, and that leaves me free to follow my own agenda.'

'Oh, I see.' She mulled things over. 'And this is a priority for you?' For the life of her she couldn't see why he would want to concentrate his attention on the ambulance service. 'Wouldn't A and E be best served if you were to concentrate on using your talents there?'

He frowned. 'I was brought in here to make changes that would benefit the department, and I believe in taking a wider view of things. I'm looking to put together a team of first responders, highly skilled doctors who go to the scene of serious accidents and make a major difference to what might otherwise be a bad outcome.'

She wasn't convinced that would be feasible. 'Most A and E doctors don't have experience of attending incidents as such. They're happy working within the department, where the environment is good and they have all the equipment they need to hand. Aren't you expecting too much of people?'

'That could be the case, perhaps, if they have no training, but that's the whole point of giving everyone the opportunity to see what it's like out there. Everyone will take a turn, and I don't see that there's any time like the present to make a start...though, of course, I understand that you have a lot of pressure on you right now. If you don't feel you can manage it, I'll have to make other arrangements.'

'I didn't say that.' She frowned. Her life was difficult enough at the moment, with so many changes taking place, the move down here, a new job, her stepfather and the worry about her aunt's health all playing on her mind. She could have coped with the routine of day-to-day work, but she was definitely put out by the sudden turnabout in what was expected of her.

It wouldn't do to admit her apprehensions to him, though, would it? More than likely he would simply pounce on any weakness and it would be one more black mark against her. She braced herself.

'I'm not exactly dressed for the occasion,' she told him, glancing down at her smart skirt and cotton top, 'and, to be honest, I wouldn't have thought you were either.' Was he really willing to mess up that elegant suit?

To her surprise, he grinned. 'You're quite right,' he acknowledged. His expression was relaxed and she was startled by the change in him. She couldn't help noticing his well-shaped mouth and the strong, angular line of his jaw.

She looked away. All of a sudden, he was far too good-looking for her peace of mind.

'We'd better go and change into paramedics outfits,' he added, walking to the door. 'I'll show you where they're stored. This way.' He indi-cated a route along the corridor, swivelled around and set off at a brisk pace, clearly expect-ing her to jump to it.

Taken by surprise, she struggled to keep up with him. The man was an anomaly, not at all like the consultant she had envisaged. She had a horrible feeling that he was a clone of her step-father in the making, though without Evan's spite, she conceded, but absolutely someone used to having everything his own way without question.

They kitted up in a short time, and were ready for the first callout when it came. The para-medics, Tim and Jack, were both thoroughly competent professionals, she discovered, though they were quick with the banter when they first met up.

'You're new,' Jack murmured, looking her over with appreciation. 'Pretty, too. My day just got better.'

'I saw her first,' Tim said. 'Out of the way, loser.'

Kayleigh smiled, and hoped that Lewis wouldn't take it amiss. She needn't have worried. He simply shook his head, treating the pair of them with mocking disdain.

They went out to a skateboarding park, where a teenager had had the misfortune to come off a ramp and smash into two others. There were ankle injuries, a broken collar-bone and a head trauma.

Her boss was in his element, she noticed, when it came to dealing with their patients. He took stock of the situation and moved in to assess and resuscitate his patient within moments. Kayleigh was very much an outsider, unaccustomed to the chaos of an accident scene, but she did what she could to assist and smooth the transit to hospital.

Later in the day she found she was more comfortable with how things were done, and Lewis pushed her more to the forefront of things, so that when they were called to a road traffic accident, she was the first to hurry over to a small child who lay by the side of the road.

'They were playing football in the street and he ran out after the ball,' a neighbour said. 'The driver of the car had no chance. He slammed on his brakes, but it was too late and he hit him. The poor lad went flying into the air.'

Kayleigh knelt down beside the child. His mother crouched nearby, wiping tears away from her face. 'I think it's his leg,' she said, struggling to keep her voice level. 'I think he banged his head as well, and he was very still and quiet after it happened. I know he's in a lot of pain.'

Kayleigh did her best to reassure the mother and the little boy. He was about seven years old, and he was a pitiful sight, one that wrenched her heart. He wasn't saying anything, but he was conscious and his eyes looked frightened.

'Matt, I just want to check you over to see how you're doing.' She made a swift examination, and it soon became clear that he had a broken thighbone.

'We'll splint that,' Lewis said in a low voice, 'and support his head so that there's no movement when we transfer him to the ambulance. I don't think there's a major head injury, but we need to be sure. There could be abdominal trauma as well. Do you want to see to the splint while I give him an injection of pain-killer?'

Kayleigh nodded. 'We're going to try to make you more comfortable,' she told Matt. 'Dr McAllister will give you something to take away the pain, and then we'll get you into the ambulance and take you to hospital.'

Tim took the boy's mother to one side and explained the procedure. 'It looks like a displaced fracture,' he told her, 'which means that the bones have been pushed out of line. He'll probably need to go for surgery in order to realign them. I should think he'll need to stay in hospital for a few days, so if you want to gather together some of his belongings, you can bring them with you to the hospital.'

'All right, I'll do that.' She touched her son's arm. 'I'll go and get your things, Matt, but I'll be back in a minute, I promise.'

The boy seemed to understand, and Kayleigh worked with Lewis to try to soothe the child's pain and get him into the ambulance. Lewis was gentle with the boy, explaining everything to him as they worked and making sure that he was at ease with what they were doing.

'You've been very brave,' Lewis told him.

'You're a star. I bet you're a great football player. Do you play in a team at school?'

'We play after school,' Matt said.

'You're a striker, I'll bet?'

'Yes.'

Kayleigh watched as the boy's lips moved in a vestige of a smile, and now she looked at Lewis with different eyes. Where she was concerned he was cool and professional, but his manner was totally different with this boy. He certainly knew how to draw the child's attention away from what was happening.

A small crowd had gathered in the street to watch them, but the people moved to one side as Jack and Lewis trundled the boy on a stretcher towards the ambulance.

Once the boy and his mother were safely inside the vehicle, and the doors had closed on them and the paramedic, Kayleigh stood back and watched the driver start up the engine.

'I always wanted to work with children at some point in my career,' she said, 'but I'm not so sure about that these days. It's hard to see them looking so poorly.'

'It's always going to be a problem if you're

any kind of a doctor. This sort of accident happens a lot in the summer months, when children are out and about. It sounds harsh, but you get used to it after a while. You have to try in some way to detach yourself.'

He might be telling her that as her boss, but she didn't think that he managed to do it. She had seen him with the boy, and he was everything that was compassionate and caring, in the same way that he had been with her aunt.

She looked around, seeing the way the houses were huddled together in a crowded terrace, with small front gardens and narrow pathways between each block.

'There's nowhere for the children to play around here, is there?' she said as she and Lewis walked back to the car. 'You can't blame them for wanting to kick a ball around, even though there's traffic passing through. They must take their lives in their hands every day.'

He sent her an oblique glance, his expression faintly teasing. 'You were obviously privileged, with a caring family and living where you did throughout your childhood. How many people have the advantage of a big house and garden, close to fields and a hop and a skip away from the sea? That's some heritage.'

'Yes, I suppose it is.' She sent him a curious glance. 'Didn't you have anything similar?'

'I don't remember anything that was particularly great.' His mouth made a straight line. He slid into the driver's seat and waited while she buckled up. Then he turned the key in the ignition and she studied him as he moved the car away from the street, heading for the road back to the hospital. That had been an odd statement for him to make.

'Right now you don't seem to have a place to call your own,' she observed quietly. 'Otherwise you wouldn't be staying in a friend's house.'

'That's true enough. This job came up and I didn't have anywhere to live, and John offered me a place to stay. He's away for a couple of months at least, so I have no worries about that for the moment. I was living in hospital accommodation before that.'

'Are you looking for a house? This job is permanent, isn't it?'

'As permanent as you get these days. I'm not actually looking for a place just yet, though I suppose I'll have to get around to it some time. I seem to have other concerns right now.'

It was strange that he had nowhere solid to call his own, almost as though he lived a nomadic kind of existence, like a drifter. None of it fitted with his obvious status as a consultant, and she was puzzled.

'What about your parents? Don't they live around here? Would staying with them be an option?'

He gave a short, harsh laugh, and she looked at him oddly. 'Did I say something wrong?' she ventured. 'I know I let my mouth run away with me sometimes.'

'You do, don't you?' He made a grimace. 'The fact is, I haven't seen my parents in a long time.'

'Oh. I'm sorry.'

'Don't be. They're not your parents and if I had a problem I would do something about it.'

She blinked. That all sounded very final and very abrupt. She wondered if his family lived in some other part of the country, but it looked as though he was finding her comments intrusive, so she decided she had better back off.

They turned onto the main road. 'Have you

decided what you're going to do about the house?' he asked. 'I know your aunt does her best to manage—she's been living there for a year or so now, hasn't she?'

'That's right. She moved in with my mother when things started to go wrong with Evan. My mother filed for divorce, and he didn't take kindly to that, but between them they managed to get him out. My aunt can be fearsome when she sets her mind to it.'

'I can imagine that.' His mouth made a crooked shape. 'I thought she looked such a picture, marching up to your stepfather with a broom the other day. You have to admire her.' He paused. 'She's obviously a spirited soul, but the truth is, she's not the woman she once was. The walk down to the shops every day wears her out. I have a feeling that this heart problem is not going to go away, and it could turn out to be a quandary for both of you.'

She nodded, her eyes troubled. 'Yes, I realise that. I could arrange for her to have the groceries delivered to the door, and it won't be a problem to buy her a little car so that she can get out and about—I just don't know whether she would accept that kind of help. She's always been very independent. Perhaps I'll just have to present it to her as a done deal.'

'And the house? I noticed you didn't answer my question.' He shot her a glance, his expression quizzical. 'Is that going to be sold over her head as a done deal as well? Though I suppose there's a fly in the ointment as far as that's concerned, isn't there?'

She stiffened. 'What do you mean?'

He drew the car into their parking slot alongside the ambulance bay at the hospital and cut the engine. 'Doesn't your stepfather have a say in what happens as well? He did say that the divorce hadn't gone through.'

'No, but the paperwork had. He doesn't have a claim on the house.'

'He seems to think differently. Didn't he say that he would see you in court?'

Her mouth made a wry twist. 'He did. I suppose I'll just have to deal with that situation when it happens.'

He sat back in his seat and looked searchingly at her face. 'You really don't like anything about him, do you?'

'Not particularly, no.' She was rigid in her seat, warding off his comments as though they were barbed arrows aimed at a sitting target, but to be fair to him, maybe he had her aunt's interests at heart. She yielded a fraction, letting her shoulders slump. 'I tried to like him, for my mother's sake, and at the beginning that wasn't hard to do. He was charming and plausible, but it wasn't too long before I began to see through the act he was putting on. Around my mother his manner was pure honey but, then, he had a lot at stake where she was concerned. She was a wealthy woman. I'm pretty certain that was the reason he married her.'

'That's a harsh judgment.' He was watching her, his eyes narrowed.

'Yes, it is.' She accepted that he would find it so. After all, he didn't know very much at all about her stepfather, and as far as he was concerned, Evan's temper the other day might have been justified. 'The thing is, the act would slip sometimes when he was alone with my sister, Heather, and me. We saw what he was really like. Heather, especially, was always at loggerheads with him. She was only seventeen, quite a few years younger than me and volatile.'

'So…what happened? Did you set out to break up the marriage?'

She sucked in a harsh breath. Shocked, she stared at him, her grey eyes troubled. 'Is that what you really think of me, that I'm capable of such a thing?'

He shrugged. 'I'm just telling it like I see it. Your aunt said you helped to get him out. I'm not judging you, one way or the other. I accept that people move things to their own ends. I'm sure that I do the same when something is important to me.'

Was he really as cool and unemotional as he seemed to suggest? He was championing her aunt's cause well enough, but perhaps that was because he had come to know her over the last few months. With everything else he appeared somehow detached.

He was a mystery to her. He hadn't been at all concerned about the effect of his actions on her when he'd plunged her without warning into working with the ambulance crew. Neither did he seem to care that he hadn't seen anything of his parents in recent years. What kind of person didn't keep in touch with their family?

'I know what you think of me,' she said, 'but you're wrong. First of all you assumed that I neglected my aunt, and now you think that I wrecked my mother's marriage, but I didn't. I tried to shield her, to protect her and prevent her from being hurt, but in the end she came to see Evan for what he was, and it was her decision to end it.'

She straightened. 'As to the house, I don't think I can, in all conscience, sell it without Heather's agreement, and I really don't know how I'm going to obtain that, when I don't have any idea where to find her.'

His gaze narrowed on her. 'You could still sell, if you put her part of the proceeds from the sale into a bank account.'

She frowned. That idea didn't appeal at all. 'Is that what you would do?'

'Maybe.' He tapped his fingers on the steering-wheel. 'But, then, I don't have any brothers or sisters, so I don't have any of the emotional baggage that goes along with that kind of dilemma.'

'You're right…you don't.' He didn't relate to his family at all from the sound of things, so what would he know about the ethics of selling a house that had been in the family for generations? Why was she even bothering to discuss it with him?

He was simply her boss, who also happened to be the bothersome man living next door. There was no escaping him.

CHAPTER THREE

HARRASSED, Kayleigh checked over the patient's chart and handed it back to the junior doctor. 'You should do an immediate CT scan,' she told him. 'We can't be sure that there hasn't been a bleed into the head, and he may need surgery, so you should bring in a neurosurgeon for a consultation.'

'Thanks, Kayleigh,' Rob said. 'I don't know what I would have done without your help. It's just that everyone is so busy...the registrar is working on a cardiac arrest and Lewis is with a patient in Intensive Care. I didn't like to have to bother you.'

'You shouldn't worry about that,' she told him. 'You're new to emergency work and it can be a bit daunting at first, to say the least. We all seem to be rushed off our feet, but it shouldn't put you off. You shouldn't be afraid to ask for help any time.'

'I won't. Thanks again.' He moved away, going in search of his patient.

Kayleigh turned back to her charts. She liked Rob. He was easygoing and always ready with a friendly word or two, and that made working life so much more pleasant.

The trouble was, there was no let-up in the number of patients to be seen, and the staff were feeling the pressure day after day. At least Lewis had limited the number of days that they were to go out with the ambulance crew to one a week. That had given her some time to get used to the way the department operated. She frowned, and rubbed at her forehead absently, trying to ease a knot of tension that had gathered there. It was a difficult job, working with trauma cases, and somewhere along the line something had to give.

'Have you signed off the asthma patient yet?' Lewis asked, coming over to the desk where she was busy writing up charts. He looked pleased with himself, and he was humming a tune under his breath.

Kayleigh glanced at him. 'No, I haven't. She's

been taken over to X-Ray because I think she may have a chest infection.'

'And the kidney stone?'

'The kidney stone is still firmly in place,' she said in a curt voice, a little more sharply than she had intended. 'The patient with the kidney stone is on his way to the renal unit.'

His mouth curved. 'OK, I guess I deserved that.' He studied her for a moment or two. 'You look out of sorts...is anything wrong?'

She slapped a chart down on the pile. 'Well, now, let's see...where do I begin?' She marked the points off on her fingers. 'I'm running tests on ten patients at a time, one of whom has just gone into convulsions in the MRI room, and then there are the dozen or so injured people we've dealt with who came in after a road traffic accident. Some of them are still waiting for X-rays. In the meantime, we're running short on blood supplies, and the obstetrician is busy in Theatre and can't get away to come and see my patient who has been haemorrhaging. Other than that, I'd say we were just fine.'

He winced. 'Just another routine day in the department, then?' He laid a hand lightly on her shoulder and turned her around. 'What you need is coffee.'

Her skin heated where his fingers had rested, sending ripples of sensation along her arm. She tried to ignore her body's hectic response. She wasn't herself. She had no control over how her nervous system reacted. 'I can't take time out for coffee. Didn't you hear any of what I just said?'

'Every word of it.' He was thoughtful. 'Perhaps we should add a cream cake as well. I've noticed that lack of sustenance makes you fractious.'

'I'll pass on the cream cake, thank you.' She made a face. 'If you had your way, I've no doubt I would end up fat as well as fractious.'

His mouth tilted at the corners. 'I expect you'd soon work it off.' He ran his glance over her assessingly. 'Anyway, you look just fine to me. A little extra weight wouldn't hurt. It would just add to the curves.'

Warm colour washed into her cheeks under his probing scrutiny. 'This may be amusing to you,' she said tightly, 'but I can tell you that all of us here are run off our feet. Whatever new ideas you have in mind for the department, perhaps you should sort out something to ease the staff situation first and foremost.'

She turned away from him to go on dealing with her paperwork, but not before she caught the swift arch of his dark brow. She tensed. Of course, she shouldn't have had a go at him that way. Why on earth didn't she learn to hold her tongue?

She waited for the recriminations to start, but instead he flattened his hand against the base of her spine and urged her away from the desk in the direction of the staff rest room.

'I told you...we're too busy...' she said, but she may as well have saved her breath.

'I know, and I'm on it. I've asked Adam to work the afternoon shift, and Tracey is coming in within the next half-hour. As to the obstetrician, I saw her stepping out of the lift just a moment ago, so I imagine she's come to take over from the nurse. So, you see, you can take a break for a few minutes.'

He sat her down at the table in the rest room and pushed a mug of coffee towards her. Then he foraged in the fridge and brought out a box of cakes, sliding chocolate éclairs and iced cream buns on to a plate.

'Comfort food,' he said. 'You certainly look as though you could do with some. Tuck in. I bought enough for everyone.' He helped himself to one of the buns.

She looked at him from under her lashes. He polished the bun off in a few mouthfuls, and then licked the cream from his fingers. He obviously never had any trouble with his weight. He was lean and fit, and he was so full of vitality that he probably burned off the energy as fast as he consumed it.

She said slowly, 'I'm sorry if I spoke out of turn. It's just that we're all under pressure.'

He nodded. 'I know that. I'm doing my best to recruit more specialist nurses, so that we can set up a minor injuries unit to be led by the nursing staff. It's all a question of triage, really, but it should eventually help to ease the burden on the A and E department.'

'That sounds like a good idea…the sooner the better.' She sipped at her coffee and succumbed to temptation, biting into one of the éclairs.

Watching her, his mouth twitched at the

corners. 'You'll feel much better now, take my word for it.'

'If you say so.' She licked cream from around her mouth with the tip of her tongue.

'I thought you looked more than a little stressed,' he commented. 'Is it more than just the job? How have things been going at home? Has there been any more trouble from your stepfather—I thought I saw his car outside the house yesterday.'

'Yes, you're right. He was there. He wanted to take some pieces from the house that he said belonged to him. I wasn't sure where they had come from, so I agreed to it.' She sighed. 'I suppose I ought to see the solicitor and set a date for when his visits are to come to an end, otherwise I can see this going on for a long time to come.'

Lewis nodded. 'I think I agree with that. It must be difficult for you, not knowing when he's going to turn up.'

She nodded. 'It's upsetting for Aunt Jane. She's not been doing very well lately—I expect you know that, anyway. I know she talks to you most days. I see you in the garden, chatting to one another.' She still hadn't got around to having the fence mended.

'That's true. I heard that she had been to see her doctor, but I don't know whether she's had the results of the tests yet.'

'We haven't heard from the specialist, but I did sneak a look at the ECG, and it looks as though there's an atrial fi-brillation, along with atrial flutter from time to time. The consultant has increased the dosage of her medication, and I think he's considering treatment to thin her blood, but he needs to do more tests first.'

'That's more or less what we expected, isn't it?'

She nodded. She felt comfortable, sitting there with him this way, and that surprised her, because up to now she had been on edge whenever he was around. The trouble was, she was all too aware of him, so that her defence systems were constantly on the alert, and that was very wearing.

She made a wry smile. Perhaps he was right about comfort food. It helped to soothe her nerves and provide a shot of adrenaline, and for a moment or two it even made her forget that most men were not to be trusted. Right now, he was a wolf in sheep's clothing. Give it time, and she had no doubt that he would bare his teeth.

There was a knock on the door and one of the nurses came into the room. 'There's been a fire at a block of flats,' she said. 'We're getting casualties coming in—sorry to interrupt your break, but you're needed out here.'

'That's all right. We're on our way.' Lewis got to his feet, and Kayleigh followed, hastily swallowing the last dregs of her coffee.

She worked alongside Lewis as they attended to the people from the fire. He checked his patient's airway and Kayleigh quickly put in an endotracheal tube to help the woman breathe more easily. When they had finished treating her, they moved on to help a teenage boy who was suffering from a burn injury to his arm.

'He says his name is Craig,' the paramedic said. 'He won't give us any more information than that, except to say that he's sixteen. We think he must have run away from home, because he isn't telling us where we can contact his parents, and the flat where he was living belongs to his friend. The friend isn't talking either.'

'That's unfortunate,' Kayleigh murmured. 'How did the fire start, Jack, do you know?'

Lewis was busy cutting away what was left of Craig's charred shirt so that he could cool the area of the burn with saline. Then he calculated the extent of the burn before administering fluids while Kayleigh put in an intravenous line and gave the boy morphine to take away the pain.

'We're not sure, but we think some children might have been playing with matches down in the basement,' Jack said. 'They managed to get out before the fire started, because they were nowhere to be seen afterwards, but there was some smouldering debris left down there. Someone called the fire brigade, but the fire spread to the upper floor before they arrived. This lad was trapped, but apparently he managed to jump to safety onto an awning. It broke his fall and helped to put out the flames on his shirt.'

Kayleigh grimaced. She looked at the teenager. 'I know it doesn't seem that way, right now, Craig,' she told him, 'but it appears as though you've been quite lucky. Things could have been far worse.'

Lewis agreed. 'You might escape with minimal scarring,' he said. 'These are partial-thickness burns, and I know they're very painful, but providing we can keep out any infection you should heal up well, given time. We'll send you to our burns unit once we're satisfied that we've done everything we can for you here.' He studied him. 'We really need to contact your parents, you know. I'm sure they'll be very concerned about you. Can you give us a phone number so that we can talk to them?'

'They don't need to know,' Craig said. 'I'll be all right. You can fix me up, can't you? That's all that needs to happen.'

Lewis didn't push the matter, but Kayleigh was still concerned. 'We can try to smooth things over for you with your parents if there's a problem,' she said. 'You don't have to face them on your own if you're in trouble of any kind.'

'I'm not in trouble.' The boy said it defiantly enough, but there was an anguished look in his eyes, as though he was holding something back, and Kayleigh instinctively sensed that inside he was just a child crying out for love. She wanted to reach out to him and comfort him but, of course, she couldn't do that. Ethically, it wouldn't have been right.

'Try to get some rest,' she said. 'I'll see if your friend is around. Do you want to see him?'

'Yes, please. I think he had cuts from smashing a window so that we could get out. I don't think he was burned.'

'That's right,' Lewis said. 'I'm sure I saw him being treated in one of the cubicles.'

Kayleigh went to find the boy. It turned out that he was slightly older than Craig, and when she saw him he was with a junior doctor who was putting stitches in a gash on his arm. The boy looked pale through loss of blood.

As soon as his treatment was completed, she took him over to Craig's cubicle and left them alone together.

'Is there anything we can do to find his parents?' she asked Lewis. 'It worries me to think of him all alone in the world.'

'You're way too soft for your own good,' Lewis murmured, shooting her a glance as he wrote up laboratory request forms. 'I'm sure he'll get by well enough. He's old enough to be living on his own.'

'Barely…and only with his parents' consent. Don't you care that he's a runaway?'

He gave a negligent shrug. 'What good would it do for me to sympathise with him? It won't solve anything, will it? All we can do is ask the police to check missing persons' reports. Social Services might want to get involved, but I doubt it, since he's sixteen and he's already found somewhere to stay. They're overrun with work as it is.'

How could he be so detached? 'It could all be just a mistake,' she said, 'a misunderstanding, or an argument that blew up over nothing. His friend told me that Craig's mother had problems and that Craig didn't get on with her boyfriend. For all we know, his mother might be desperate to have him back.'

'Then she'll have filed a report with the police.' He studied her thoughtfully. 'You have to let go, Kayleigh. It's a tough world out there and people have to learn to cope or go under…even young people like Craig.' He frowned. 'Espe-cially people like Craig. Family breakdowns happen. You should know that.'

Kayleigh shook her head. 'I don't know how you can be so unmoved by his plight. He's young, and he's in pain, and he needs his family around him.' She would never understand what made this man tick. He was in a caring profession, and yet at times he seemed so aloof from the suffering all around him.

'We can deal with his pain and his physical injuries. What we can't do is provide a panacea for all the world's ills. You should come to terms with that or you'll drain yourself dry.'

A wave of frustration washed through her and she pressed her lips together. 'I have to do something,' she said. 'I'll go and talk to the police myself.'

She walked away and went to have a word with the police officer who was in Reception, waiting to take statements from anyone who had been at the block of flats. He agreed to check the reports back at the station, and then she went off in search of her next patient.

'There's a man with a broken arm in cubicle three,' Sharon, the triage nurse told her. 'He rescued a little girl from the building and then a beam cracked and fell on him when he went back to see if anyone else was inside. He must be a very brave man to have attempted to do that.'

'It certainly sounds like it.' She took the chart that the nurse handed to her. 'Did everyone get out of the building safely?'

Sharon nodded. 'From what I heard, yes.'

'That's a relief.' Kayleigh smiled, and then glanced down at the chart. Her brows met. 'It says here that his name is Jacob Darby—is that right? He's the same age as me, twenty-seven?'

'That's right. Is there something wrong?' Sharon looked at her carefully, then glanced over her shoulder at the chart.

'No…nothing's wrong…except I think I know him.' Kayleigh was taken aback. 'If I'm right, he's my sister's ex-boyfriend.'

'Are you OK to deal with him? Do you want me to find someone else to treat him?'

Kayleigh shook her head. 'No, there's no need. It'll be fine. It was just a shock, that's all. I'm all right now.'

She went into the cubicle and looked at the patient who was sitting on the bed, his arm supported by a backslab and held in a sling.

'Jacob?' Her gaze travelled over his familiar features and took in the sun-streaked brown hair that was dusted with soot from the fire. 'I can't believe it's you...I just heard about what you did, saving that little girl. That was such a wonderful thing to do.' She hesitated and then ventured, 'I had no idea that you were living locally.'

'I went away for a while, but then came back. Everything seemed strange after Heather left. It's been three years now, and I still can't get her out of my head.' Jacob's expression was rueful, and at the same time he was gritting his teeth through the pain of his broken arm. 'She broke off with me and I haven't seen her since.'

'I'm so sorry.' She hurried over to him. 'Here, let me take a look at you. Is your pain medication wearing off?' She checked his distal pulses.

''Fraid so. They say I've broken both bones in the forearm. I put my arm up to protect myself and the beam hit me.'

'It's perhaps just as well that you did, otherwise you might have had a nasty head injury.' She studied the X-rays. 'There are the fracture lines, see? I'll call for the orthopaedic surgeon to take a look at you. We're going to have to give you an anaesthetic so that we can get the bones back into position.' She was reaching for the phone as she spoke.

'I thought you might.'

'It's an open wound, so we need to give you intravenous antibiotics and tetanus cover,' she said, coming back to him. She touched his good arm lightly. 'It's so good to see you again, Jacob. It has been such a while since we last met up. I had hoped that you might come to see us.'

'I couldn't do that, not after the way Evan went for me. I didn't want to cause any of you any more trouble.'

She leaned over and hugged him, taking care not to go anywhere near his broken arm. 'You wouldn't have done that…and Evan doesn't live at the house any more, so there are no worries on that account. It's such a relief to see you. I just wish it wasn't under these circumstances.'

There was a noise from behind her as the curtain of the cubicle was swished back and Lewis walked in.

'Is everything all right in here?' he asked, looking from one to the other.

Kayleigh straightened up, warmth creeping into her cheeks. What must he think of her, getting so close to a patient?

'Yes, of course,' she said. 'I need to send

Jacob to Theatre for a reduction of his fracture. The orthopaedic surgeon is waiting for him in Theatre Two.'

'So I heard. He's just finished working on a hip dislocation.' He was checking the X-rays as he spoke. 'I'll help you to take him up there.'

'Thanks.' Kayleigh turned to Jacob. 'You've suffered a nasty fracture and the bones will probably need to be fixed in place with a metal plate. We'll need to take more X-rays to check that all's well before we finish up and put the arm in a cast.' She frowned. 'I'm afraid you're going to be off work for a while.'

His green eyes were resigned. 'It had to happen at the height of the season. We always get a lot more people signing on for sports instruction in the summer. Still, it can't be helped, I suppose.'

Lewis wheeled him towards the lift bay. 'You work at the leisure centre?'

'That's right.' Jacob leaned back against his pillows and it was plain to see that his pain level was increasing.

The surgeon was already scrubbing in, and Kayleigh said goodbye to Jacob before leaving him in the hands of the anaesthetist. 'I'll come and look in on you later,' she said.

'I gather you and Jacob know each other fairly well.' Lewis murmured, glancing at Kayleigh as they walked back to the lifts.

She returned his gaze. 'That's right. How did you know?'

'You mean, apart from the fact that you were hugging him?' His mouth twisted. 'The nurse told me. She said you were thrown when you saw his chart, so I stopped by to see if anything was wrong.'

The lift doors swished open and they stepped inside. No one else was waiting, and he pushed the button to take them back down to ground level.

'Everything was fine,' Kayleigh said, 'but it was a shock, seeing him out of the blue, like that. He and my sister were inseparable at one time. I thought something might come of their relationship, but it all ended badly.'

She was troubled, remembering how it had been, and he studied her pale features and asked, 'What happened? It looks as though it still has the power to upset you, even now.'

'It does. My stepfather didn't take to Jacob.

He thought he was too old for my sister, and he did what he could to stop them from seeing each other. He and Heather used to have some furious rows about it, but the last one was too much for her. She left one night without saying a word to anyone and we haven't seen her since. That was three years ago.'

'I'm sorry. Hasn't there been any kind of contact since then?'

'There were a couple of postcards.' Her mouth wavered. 'I think she felt bad about leaving Mum, but she wasn't ever going to come back while Evan was around. Somehow the cards made it worse. She...she sounded so forlorn, and we had no way of getting in touch. There was no forwarding address.'

He put his hands on her, holding her gently, his fingers cupping her shoulders and lending support. 'Couldn't you have checked out the postmark?'

She gazed at him, her eyes bright with unshed tears. 'Of course. Do you think we didn't try?' Why would he assume that?

She pulled in a shuddery breath. 'We think she had someone post them for her, someone who was travelling around, or else she was constantly on the move. Whenever we followed it up, the trail had gone cold. She must have gone from place to place. She doesn't want to be found.'

Through the thin fabric of her top, she felt his fingers lightly massaging her soft flesh, creating warm, soothing whirlpools of sensation. It was an alluring, mesmeric feeling, one that made her want to draw closer to him and allow herself to be folded into his arms.

'You can't be sure about that,' he said. 'Anyway, I expect she'll come back when she's good and ready.'

The feeling of warmth dropped away from her and she stared up at him, a glitter of frustration coming into her eyes. How could he be so glib about something that was so painful to her?

'After all this time? Somehow, I doubt it.'

The lift came to a standstill, and he released her, letting his hands fall by his sides. 'No wonder you were so taken up with the plight of the teenage runaway,' he murmured. 'You identify with him because of your sister.'

Maybe that was true...but what had his

answer been to that dilemma? *You have to let go,* he had said... *Family breakdowns happen.* A cold sense of dismay washed through her. He would never understand what she was going through, would he? It simply wasn't in his psyche.

CHAPTER FOUR

KAYLEIGH knocked for a minute or two longer at the front door of the house next door, before finally giving up. Lewis wasn't answering. So what ought she do now? Aunt Jane wouldn't be very happy with her if she simply abandoned the mission.

She glanced down at the casserole dish in her hand. Somehow or other this had to be delivered, and it had to be done quickly, too, as she was supposed to be on duty in less than an hour.

She walked around the house to the back. This was a much smaller property than her own, white-painted in a similar fashion, though some of the paintwork was beginning to peel off, and when she looked up at the roof she saw that one or two of the slates needed fixing.

The back door was open, presumably to let in

some fresh air on what promised to be a beautiful summer's day, though a small grey cat shot past her from the garden as she looked about, and maybe it had been left open for him.

'Hello,' she called out, following the cat into the kitchen. 'Lewis, are you there?'

He wasn't in the kitchen, and she stood and looked around her, taking in the smell of fresh paint. It was clear that Lewis had been busy in there, because the walls were a light-reflecting magnolia colour, and the skirting-boards and doorframes were gleaming. She couldn't help but notice the clean, uncluttered sweep of the work surfaces. The interior door was open and she could see through the gap to another room. It might have been a dining room, but there wasn't much furniture in there and the wallpaper looked as though it was coming away from the wall in places. He obviously hadn't got around to decorating that room just yet.

She started towards the doorway, but stopped as the grey bundle of fur wrapped itself around her bare legs, arching its back in a sensuous movement. Then the cat stepped away from her a little, looking up at her expectantly, his tail carried high in the air. Putting the casserole dish down onto a wooden, scrubbed pine table, she knelt to stroke the animal.

'I know what you're after,' she told him, tickling his ears. 'You can smell the food, can't you?'

He made a purring sound, almost as though he was echoing her thoughts and adding along with it a determined plea for sustenance.

'Sorry lad,' she murmured. 'I can't help you there, not right at this moment.'

'Don't pay any heed to Moggie. He's always making out that he's hungry. He's a con artist.' Kayleigh was startled to hear Lewis's deep voice coming to her out of the blue, and she quickly straightened up.

'I'm looking after him while John's away,' Lewis added, 'and he's making the most of it. As far as he's concerned, the only important things in life are eating and sleeping, with maybe the odd tummy rub thrown in for good measure.'

Kayleigh glanced across the room at him. 'Sounds like the...' She broke off, her eyes widening, her mouth dropping open in mid-sentence. 'Ultimate hedonist,' she finished, then clamped her mouth shut and simply stared.

He must have just come from the shower, because he was wearing dark grey trousers that rested loosely on his lean hips, and other than that he was bare-chested, showing off a naked, perfectly flat abdomen and a six-pack that any athlete would be proud of. His skin was smooth and lightly bronzed, faintly glistening, and for an utterly mad moment the blood rushed to her head and she wondered what it would be like to run her fingers over his shoulders and down those strong arms.

She blinked and quickly tried to gather herself together, hoping that her cheeks didn't look as hot as they felt. 'I came to bring you an offering from my aunt,' she managed. 'It's a hotpot that she thought you might like for your supper. She's convinced you're starving yourself, living here without a woman to look after you…the days of equality and men looking after themselves haven't quite made an impact on Aunt Jane yet.' She gave a quick shake of her head. 'Perhaps you could leave it in the fridge and heat it up later, in the oven. She's a really good cook. I'm sure you'll enjoy it.' She paused to take a breath and realised that she had been babbling.

'That was thoughtful of her. I appreciate her doing that for me,' he murmured. He was rubbing at his damp hair with a towel, watching her with a quizzical expression, and Kayleigh observed inconsequentially that water droplets had lent an iridescent gleam to his black hair. His brows were straight and dark, too, and she wondered why on earth she was noticing these small details with such clarity this morning. Didn't she see him every day at work?

'Yes, well…perhaps I should go,' she murmured. She was becoming increasingly conscious of the need to escape. 'I still have to get ready for work. Aunt Jane just asked me to tell you to be sure and heat it through thoroughly. She thought about two hundred degrees centigrade ought to do it, for about twenty to twenty five minutes.'

He frowned. 'How does that translate to a microwave oven, do you know?' She looked at him in confusion and his mouth straightened. 'The cooker went kaput last week,' he explained, 'and I'm still waiting for an engineer to come out…something about a mix-up with my friend's insurance, so I might have to pay another firm to fix it for me...or buy a new cooker.' His dark brows drew together at that. 'I suppose that might be an option.'

'Um...' She gazed at him, nonplussed. 'I think the dish is probably too bulky for the microwave.' She made a crooked smile. 'My aunt always seems to prepare enough food to feed an army.' Backing away, she said hurriedly, 'Tell you what, perhaps you would do better to come over to our place to eat. Come after work... there's more than enough to go round, and it will be simpler that way.'

'OK.' He watched her retreat out of the door. 'I'll see you in A and E in a little while.'

She nodded. 'Actually, I'll be bringing my aunt in to the hospital with me, so that she can have some more tests done. They've had her wear a twenty-four-hour monitor to check her heart rate as she went about the house, and now they want to do an echo of her heart to see what's happening with the valves and so on. She's really not doing too well, and she's a bit apprehensive about it all.'

'That's perhaps understandable. She's been

healthy all her life and now things have started to go wrong. I'll have a word with her later on.'

'She'll be pleased about that.'

Kayleigh turned and fled. Had she really just invited him to dinner? Had she entirely lost her senses? The vision of his bare male torso was proving to be altogether too much for her to handle. She didn't want to be reminded of his maleness, of his perfectly honed body. Now every time she saw him dressed in a suit she would be all too conscious of the man underneath, of his stunning physique and the way the muscles rippled whenever he moved.

She hurried away to get ready for work, and a short while later, without any further incident, she arrived at the hospital with her aunt.

Aunt Jane, for her part, was relieved to see Lewis when they arrived at the A and E department. 'I'm so pleased that you'll be coming to dinner,' she told him. 'Kayleigh told me about the problem with your cooker. We can't let you live on microwave meals. You should have told me before this, and we would have made sure that you were all right...wouldn't we, Kayleigh?'

Kayleigh nodded. She couldn't bring herself to say anything just then. She was simply thankful that by now he was wearing a suit.

'You look a little shaky on your feet,' Lewis said, glancing at Aunt Jane. 'Come and sit down on the bench out in the quadrangle and rest up for a while.' He waved a hand towards an enclosed courtyard, a landscaped area to one side of the emergency unit, and when she nodded, he went to help her out there.

Aunt Jane sat down on a wooden seat and breathed in the fresh air, while all around her the flowers that crowded the stone tubs bobbed their heads in the light breeze.

'I have to go to Cardiology,' Aunt Jane told him. 'I'm OK, but I'm feeling a little nervous and it's making my heart race a bit.'

'Take it easy for a while,' he said. 'The tests are nothing for you to worry about. You won't feel a thing, I promise.'

'I know. Kayleigh explained them to me.' She patted Kayleigh's hand. She was breathless and a touch light-headed, but after a moment or two of sitting still, she seemed to recover. 'You had a dramatic day yesterday, didn't you?' she said.

'I read in the local paper about the fire at the block of flats. They said people were being brought in all afternoon, and even one of the firemen was taken to hospital and had to have a surgical procedure to help him to breathe.'

'Yes, that's right. We treated him for smoke inhalation,' Lewis told her. 'We had a bit of a race against time, because his throat tissues were swelling up and we couldn't intubate him, so we had to cut into his windpipe to help him to breathe.'

'The poor man. Is he going to be all right?'

Lewis nodded. 'He is. Do you know, to begin with, he was more concerned about a teenage runaway than he was about himself? He said he had tried to rescue him but there was a delay while they were getting the equipment in place...as it was, the boy managed to jump clear just in time.'

'The boy's a runaway? Have they found out where he's come from?'

'Not yet.' Kayleigh went and fetched a wheelchair from the covered walkway. 'Let's sit you down on this and then I'll take you over to Cardiology.'

'All right, love.' Aunt Jane allowed Kayleigh and Lewis to assist her, and then sat for a moment recovering her breath.

Lewis glanced at Kayleigh. 'How is she going to get home afterwards?'

'Our neighbour is coming to fetch her. Margaret has some shopping to do in town, and then she's going to call in here and take her back home as soon as she's ready. She'll keep an eye on her for the rest of the day.'

'That's good.' Lewis watched as they headed for the corridor. 'I'll see you later, Jane.'

Kayleigh took her aunt over to the lifts and made sure that she was being looked after in the cardiology unit. She returned to A and E some half an hour later, just as the paramedics were bringing in a middle-aged man.

'This is Adam Stonehurst,' Tim said. 'He's complaining of abdominal pain, and he's been vomiting. It seems he got into difficulties out at sea, so the air sea rescue service brought him in off his yacht, and transferred him to our ambulance at the coast. He's feverish, and it looks as though he's jaundiced as well.'

'Thanks, Tim,' Kayleigh said. 'I'll take over

from here.' She glanced at the paramedic. 'Was he alone on the yacht?'

'He had his wife and a couple of friends with him, but none of them was particularly skilled at navigation, so the coastguard people are guiding them back to shore. It was a pleasure cruiser type vessel, one that would be a little hard to handle if you didn't know what you're doing.'

'Are any of those on board suffering similar symptoms?'

Tim shook his head. 'No, it looks as though he's the only one.'

'OK, thanks again.' Kayleigh wheeled the man into a cubicle, and began to make a swift examination. 'Bear with me, Adam,' she murmured. 'I know that you're uncomfortable, but I'll be as gentle as I can.'

The man nodded, but didn't say anything, and a film of sweat broke out on his brow. Then he started to retch, Sharon hurried forward with a kidney bowl.

Kayleigh waited while he recovered from this latest bout of sickness and wondered whether Adam was a drinker. His skin was sallow, and the whites of his eyes were becoming yellow, so it was possible that his problems were the result of habitual overindulgence in alcohol. The paramedics had already questioned him about his drinking habits, but the man had not admitted to having a problem, just the normal social intake. Kayleigh wasn't exactly sure what he considered normal, because people sometimes tended to underestimate the amount they drank.

'I'm going to take some blood for testing,' she told him. 'Have you had any similar attacks before this?'

'Yes,' he managed, his face contorted with pain, 'but nothing as bad as this.'

Lewis came into the cubicle a short time later. He nodded to the patient, and then glanced briefly at Kayleigh. He said softly, 'Was your aunt all right when you left her in Cardiology? You could have stayed with her, you know, if you had wanted. We're all right down here for the time being.'

'I thought about it, but she's with the technician right now—she didn't really want me hanging around. You know, my aunt can be a very independent soul at times.'

He made a wry smile. 'Yes, I'm beginning to see that.'

He picked up the patient's chart and went to stand by him at the side of the bed. 'Hello,' he said, nodding to Adam. 'I'm Dr McAllister. I'm here to oversee your case, but I can see that Dr Byford is looking after you, so I'm sure that you'll do very well in her capable hands. I take it that your symptoms came on suddenly?'

'Yes, they did.' Adam pulled in a quick breath. 'I thought I would be all right to take the boat out—I wanted to show her off to my friends, but we'd only been at sea for around half an hour when I started to feel really ill.'

Kayleigh said quietly, 'There's a degree of abdominal ten-derness. I'm going to do some liver-function tests to see if we can find out what's going on.'

Lewis acknowledged that with a brief inclination of his head. 'Perhaps you would let me know the results as soon as you have them?'

'Of course.' She was surprised that he'd asked. Usually he made a quick check of every patient's treatment and signed off the chart, but this was something different for him, wanting to be notified as soon as they came in. Perhaps he didn't trust her judgment in this case. She frowned at that.

Lewis had already turned back to the patient. 'I've just been having a conversation with Air Sea Rescue. They tell me your yacht is a beauty. A fifty-footer with twin engines and a sundeck. You must be proud of her?'

'I am.' Adam tried a smile. 'She's just been for a refit and...' He paused as another wave of sickness hit him, and the nurse wiped a cold cloth across his forehead, then he went on, 'she has a new galley and new upholstery.'

'Then we must get you back on your feet so that you can show her off properly.' Lewis gave him an encouraging smile. 'We have to wait for the test results to come back, but we'll give you supportive treatment in the meantime to help to make you feel more comfortable.'

'Thanks.' Adam leaned back against his pillows and closed his eyes. He was clearly exhausted.

Kayleigh stopped to speak to the nurse for a moment about her patient's care, and then she followed Lewis out of the cubicle.

She caught up with him by the desk. 'You

seem to be quite sympathetic towards this patient…do you have a particular reason for being concerned about this case?'

'There's no real reason…it's just an area where I have an interest. I suppose you could say that I tend to be more than usually on the alert whenever a person with liver problems comes in.'

'Why is that? Is it because liver damage can't be reversed once it has reached a certain stage? I would have thought that could apply to any number of other organs in the body. At least with liver damage, the problem can be halted in its tracks if the patient is a drinker and takes heed early enough.'

'Are you assuming that's his problem?'

'No… Obviously, I have to wait for the test results before I can be sure of anything, but it's a possibility, isn't it?'

'That's true, but there's nothing in his history to suggest alcohol as a cause. It could be all manner of things.' His mouth made a rueful line. 'Disease is no respecter of wealth and status. Our yachtsman is as vulnerable as any other person to ill health.'

His expression was brooding, and she looked at him thoughtfully for a while. 'It looks as though you identify with this man in some way, or is it the sailing that's a common interest?'

His mouth curved. 'I do know something about sailing. I worked as a deckhand on chartered cruisers in my summer vacations for a few years running. It was a great feeling, taking the boats out for a spin over the water. I had a friend who knew all about handling yachts and he taught me all I needed to know. They were good times.' He looked at her. 'You were quite the sailor yourself, weren't you? Your aunt told me snippets from time to time about the way you spent your childhood. She said your father had a yacht and that you were a dab hand at the wheel.'

'It was a small motor cruiser, and she's exaggerating. I didn't get to go out in the boat all that often, but it was good while it lasted. My father used to take us out as a family, and they were happy memories. Aunt Jane used to come along, too, with her husband.'

Lewis frowned. 'I noticed that she wears a ring, but she hasn't said anything to me about her marriage. I wondered if there was a divorce, or whether something happened to him.'

Kayleigh grimaced. 'Uncle Simon died with my father in a car crash. They had been out to a business meeting and were driving home to us when someone tried to overtake on the brow of a hill, coming in the opposite direction. The car smashed into them.'

'I'm sorry. That must have been awful.'

She nodded. 'Yes, it was. I was ten years old and it hit me hard. I wanted to know why no one could save them. My mother and aunt were inconsolable for a long while, but Heather was only three at the time, and I think they tried to get themselves together for her sake. I don't think she really understood what was going on.'

'Perhaps that was just as well.'

'Yes.'

The nurse came to find her just then, and Kayleigh sloughed off the memories of the past and went to attend to her patient. When the liver-function test results came back some time later, she did an ultrasound scan on the yachtsman, and then organised a liver biopsy.

'You were right,' she told Lewis, as they were

preparing to finish their shift at the end of the day. 'His problem wasn't down to drinking at all, and neither was it down to any of the usual causes of hepatitis. I don't believe I've seen a case like this before.'

'It's rare, I grant you. I had a quick peek at your notes. It looks as though he's suffering from some kind of autoimmune hepatitis. We may never know what started it off, but we'll run some more tests anyway. In the meantime, you need to start him on high-dose steroids to reduce the inflammation. We may need to add an immunosuppressant drug as well, but we'll leave that for the specialist to decide.'

'I'll set that in motion before I leave.' She sent him a quick glance. 'We'll see you at dinner, shall we?'

He nodded, and she added, 'Say, around seven o'clock? That will give me time to organise things and make sure Aunt Jane is comfortable. She wants to be hands on with everything, but she seems to be going downhill these days, and I'm always having to persuade her to take things easy.'

'It must be hard for her to take a back seat when she's been a driving force all her life.' He flicked through a patient's file. 'I have to go and organise a scan, so I'll see you later. Maybe I'll be home early enough to come and give you a hand.'

Kayleigh wasn't sure about that. It was one thing to see him at work and to liaise with one another over their patients, but the thought of being at close quarters with him in the confines of her kitchen was another matter entirely. She still hadn't properly recovered from the morning's episode.

As it was, Aunt Jane already had the meal preparations well under way when Kayleigh arrived home.

'I wanted you to rest,' Kayleigh said, glancing around the kitchen and breathing in the appetising smells coming from the oven. There were pans of vegetables simmering gently on the hob, and Aunt Jane had one of her famous suet apple puddings cooking nicely in the steamer. 'You're not well, and you should have left all this to me. I told you that I would see to it as soon as I came home.'

'But you've been at work all day,' Aunt Jane protested. 'I couldn't leave it all to you.' She laid a hand down lightly on the worktop in order to steady herself.

'You can now,' Kayleigh murmured, leading her aunt away from the cooker. 'You sit down here in the recliner and put your feet up. I'll allow you to talk to me and tell me about the hospital tests while I lay the table…if you feel up to it, that is.'

Aunt Jane looked frail, and her breathing was a little ragged, so that Kayleigh suspected she was relieved to be able to hand everything over. At least, she didn't protest very much, and when Lewis came and knocked on the door at around half past six, she didn't demur when he started to help with the preparations for the meal.

'Did you get any of your test results?' he asked, but Aunt Jane shook her head.

'No, I have to wait for those. They said if the tablets don't work, I might need to go in for a cardio something or other, to slow the heart rate down.'

'A cardioversion?'

'That sounds about right. They don't want to do that unless they have to…too intrusive, they said, but it might come to that.' She paused to get her breath. 'I'm sure I'll be fine.'

'Hmm…we'll see,' Kayleigh murmured. 'If they don't sort out your problems soon, I think I might go and have a word with the consultant, to see if we can't get things moving. It worries me to see you looking so tired and I know that your chest has been hurting.'

'I don't want you to do that, love,' Aunt Jane said. 'You worry too much.'

'Maybe, but I noticed that you're a bit unsteady on your feet, and you've already collapsed a few times.' Kayleigh turned to Lewis. 'Would you help my aunt into the dining room while I bring the serving dishes through? I thought we would eat in there as it's such a nice day. The sun streams in through the windows and it makes it a really pleasant room.'

'Of course.' Lewis was already moving to help Aunt Jane to her feet, while Kayleigh made sure that the food was set out on the dining table.

'Kayleigh said that you treated a man who was taken ill on his yacht today,' Aunt Jane said, directing her gaze towards Lewis, as they sat down and began to help themselves to food. 'Is he going to be all right?'

'I hope so. It may take a few months for him

to get back on track, but usually we can keep his type of illness under control. My father has a similar liver disease, although there were other factors that needed to be dealt with before he started on the road to recovery.'

Kayleigh glanced at him. His expression was serious, and she wondered if that was the reason he had been so keen to follow Adam's progress through every stage. He must have been reminded of his father's condition...so much so that it struck a chord with him...and yet he had said that they didn't keep in touch. That struck her as odd.

'Is that why you decided on medicine as a career?' she asked, adding new potatoes to her plate.

'Not really. I mean, I was worried about my father—I was young when he was taken ill, and for a while we didn't know if he was going to recover, so it was a traumatic time. Then we discovered that he had pernicious anaemia, which was exacerbating his problems, and once that was sorted out, the doctors started to make some headway.'

'That must have been a difficult time for you,' Kayleigh murmured.

'I suppose it was. I tried to talk to my father about how he was feeling, but he was always a very remote kind of man, and he didn't believe in showing any kind of weakness. In some ways I felt as though I was sticking my nose where it wasn't wanted , as though I shouldn't even be asking.'

'That's sad,' Aunt Jane said. 'It's a shame that he wouldn't confide in you, but perhaps he didn't realise how worried you must have been.' She paused to spear a carrot with her fork. 'So what turned you towards becoming a doctor?'

'A friend of mine was taken ill at school. He stopped breathing, and someone gave him the kiss of life and managed to keep him alive until the ambulance came. It was touch and go for a while, but he survived. It made a huge impression on me.'

'I can imagine it would.'

He smiled, then stopped to taste the casseroled meat and vegetables and said appreciatively, 'You know, this is delicious, Jane. You're a terrific cook.'

Aunt Jane's cheeks flushed with pink colour. 'Thank you.'

'You should try her apple suet pudding,' Kayleigh said. 'It melts in the mouth, it's like a little taste of heaven.'

They talked about this and that for the rest of the meal, and finally, when they were all full up and couldn't manage another morsel, Kayleigh started to clear the table. 'I'll make a pot of coffee,' she said.

'Not for me, love,' Aunt Jane said. 'I think I'd quite like to go up to my room, if you don't mind? I'm feeling rather tired. I think I'll go to bed and watch television for a while. Do you mind if I leave you to it?'

'Of course not.' Kayleigh wiped her hands on a tea towel. 'I'll help you upstairs.' She frowned. 'Perhaps we ought to think about getting a stair lift installed.'

Aunt Jane demurred at that. 'Nonsense. As soon as the doctors sort me out, I'll be just fine.'

Kayleigh helped her up to bed, and when she came back downstairs she discovered that Lewis had stacked the dishwasher, and a pot of coffee was steaming gently, filling the kitchen with its aromatic scent. He placed two coffee-cups on a tray and added a jug of cream and a pot of sugar.

'Shall we take this out onto the terrace?' he asked. 'It's still a warm evening.'

'That would be good,' she murmured. Now that she was alone with him, she was beginning to notice a fluttering sensation starting up in her abdomen and it had nothing at all to do with the meal she had just eaten. She was becoming far too aware of him, that was the trouble, and she wasn't at all sure how to handle her feelings on that score. Men had always let her down, one way or the other, and she didn't want to risk getting burned all over again.

Perhaps he detected something of her reticence, because once they were out on the terrace he concentrated his attention on pouring coffee and said carefully, 'We both seem to have gone through worrying times with our parents—our fathers, especially. Though it must have been even more difficult for you, because your stepfather came into your life, and that doesn't seem to have worked out too well either.' He glanced at her. 'I don't think you ever told me how it came about, did you? I expect your mother was lonely after your father died.'

'Yes, she was.' Kayleigh sat down at the table

and sipped at the coffee. 'She had to keep going, because she had two girls to care for and, of course, Heather was only three years old. Still, she had Aunt Jane to comfort her and offer support.' She made a wry smile. 'Heather turned to me as her big sister. We went everywhere together and there was a very strong bond between us.'

'How did she react when your stepfather came along?' He was watching her from under dark lashes, and she couldn't help noticing how relaxed he looked, leaning back in his garden chair, his long legs thrust out in front of him, the fabric of his trousers stretched taut against his thighs.

She looked away. He was far too much of a distraction. 'She was ten by the time Evan came into our lives, and my mother and he didn't get married for another two years after that. He was good to us, and he seemed to be a really nice person. I think we both took to him at first, though there was always a faint niggle at the back of my mind that he wasn't what he seemed. And, of course, when she was older, Heather never saw eye to eye with him. They argued constantly—about the clothes she wore, her make-up, her boyfriends.'

She curved her hands around her coffee-cup as though that would warm the cold fringes of her heart where pain still lurked. 'In the end, after that last fierce argument, she couldn't stand it any more, and she packed her bags and left, without saying a word to anyone. There was a note for me, telling me that she was sorry she had to leave, and one for Mum, asking her to forgive her.' Her lips began to tremble and she broke off, placing the cup carefully back down on the table.

Getting to her feet, she went over to the end of the terrace, to where there was an area of decking, raised up so that you could see right over the garden. She climbed up the wooden steps and stood by a latticed panel, looking out but not really seeing anything, her fingers resting on the handrail.

Lewis came to join her there. 'You miss her, don't you?' he said.

'Yes, I do. I've tried everything I can think of to find her, but she seems to have disappeared. None of the agencies we've been to have come across any trace of her.'

He was quiet for a moment. 'Have you tried

making some posters with her photograph and distributing them in some of the surrounding counties?'

She shook her head. 'We put her photo in a few of the local newspapers, with a piece about her, but nothing came of it.'

'Well, you might reach a wider audience that way. A newspaper article is only going to be around for one or two days, but posters can be left up for a while, especially if you get shop-keepers to agree to put them in their windows.'

She gazed at him. 'I could try that. I'll print some out and see what I can do to spread them as far afield as possible.'

'If there's anything I can do to help, let me know.'

'Thanks, I will.'

He sent her an oblique glance, coming to stand closer to her. 'Are you sure that everything was entirely your stepfather's fault? After all, most teenagers rebel against their parents' re-strictions. Perhaps Evan was just doing the best he could in the circumstances?'

She shook her head. 'I think there was more to it than that. He changed once he and my mother

were married. He went through money fast...
there was always something he wanted, a sports
car, fine clothes, holidays in exotic places.'

He laughed. 'Don't we all want those
things? You've been privileged—you've had
them all your life, and perhaps you don't see
the temptation for someone who's never had
it so good. Is it so wrong to hanker after those
things if the money's available? Your mother
couldn't have had any objection to him having
what he wanted.'

His mouth made a wry shape. 'I know it isn't
any of my business, and I'm not meaning to pry
in any way here, but for all that he liked to spend
your mother's money, it seems to me that you
haven't been left badly off. You're still wealthy
in your own right and you won't ever have to
worry about money, from what I've gathered.'

She glowered at him. Did he think she was
making a fuss about nothing? What did he know
of the way things had been when Evan had been
around? 'That's only because my father had the
foresight to make provision for us when he was
alive. He set up trust funds for my sister and me,
and for my mother. He wanted to make sure

that nothing could affect our standard of living in the future.'

'So where's the problem?'

She flashed him a look of pure frustration, her grey eyes sparking fitfully. 'How can I explain it to you? I know that Evan was taking advantage of my mother, and that he set out to do it from the first, but what would you know about any of that? Who are you to criticise?' His dark brows rose at that, but she ignored the warning signs. 'Maybe you've never been in the position of having money, and you don't understand the responsibility that goes along with it. You just think I'm a poor little rich girl, with no reason to complain, don't you?'

'Aren't you?' He moved in right beside her, and before she had any notion of what he was about to do, his hand shot out and whipped around her waist, pulling her to him in one strong movement. 'You've had it all, haven't you? And you look at me and think, what is he? A drifter, no long-term commitments, no real responsibilities, happy enough to crash at a friend's place and taking advantage of your aunt's generosity.'

His summing-up was almost shocking in its accuracy and her eyes widened. He stared down at her and his mouth tilted at the corners because he knew that his shot had hit home. He was looking at her, his expression showing a hint of mockery, but his blue eyes glinted with something else, something that in a strange way reminded her of sunlight shimmering on the sea.

His actions were a contradiction, though, his arms suddenly powerful, as he tugged her up against him, and then his head bent, his mouth coming down on hers, pressuring her, taking what he wanted, tasting her lips, and filling her with an all-consuming, hot, heavy feeling of desperate need. She didn't know what it was that she wanted, but her pulses were throbbing and the blood raced through her veins, filling her body with flame.

He deepened the kiss, crushing her lips beneath his, and in a distant part of her mind she recognised that she had never known a feeling of such intense desire before this. It bewildered her, and turned her world upside down.

When he let her go, just a second or two later,

her head was spinning, her thoughts whirling like a stormcloud that was about to burst. She stared up at him, speechless, wanting something more yet appalled by her body's treacherous response to him.

His eyelids were half-closed, his expression watchful. 'Are you all right?' he asked.

'I don't know...I'm not sure how to answer that,' she managed, finding her voice. 'What was that all about?'

He gave a negligent shrug. 'Maybe the loner in me wanted to show you that there isn't all that much difference between us. When it comes down to it, we're all just human beings, blundering our way through life.'

He straightened his shoulders. 'I should go. Thanks for the meal...and I hope your aunt is feeling better by morning.'

He walked away, and she didn't try to stop him. She was confused and out of sorts, but her overriding emotion was one of dismay. Was he totally hung up on wealth and family and the fact that they appeared to have completely different approaches to life?

Worst of all had been his reaction to that... He

hadn't kissed her because he wanted her. He had done it simply because he could, and she didn't know at all how she felt about that.

CHAPTER FIVE

'ARE you sure this is the right place?' Kayleigh slid out of the passenger seat of the fast-response car and followed Lewis across the rough ground towards the ramshackle outbuilding on the edge of a deserted farm.

'This is where the ambulance has stopped,' Lewis answered. 'Jack seemed to know where he was going. He said the farmhouse has been empty for the last six months, and he lives around here, so he should know what he's talking about.'

Kayleigh frowned. 'It doesn't make any sense. What on earth would a small boy be doing out here, of all places? Everyone else is taking advantage of the sunshine and heading for the beach.'

'Not this one, by all accounts.' Lewis covered the remaining ground in a few long strides, and Kayleigh hurried along beside him. Her shoes crunched on gravel, and she might almost have twisted her ankle in a pothole if it hadn't been for Lewis making a grab for her and steadying her.

His fingers gripped her arm in a hold that was at the same time firm and supportive and his touch had a startling effect on her, sending shockwaves rippling throughout her body. It brought back to her with full force the memory of that evening when he had kissed her, and the world had seemed to tilt on its axis. Back then, she hadn't thought she would ever be the same again, and now she had to brace herself to remember that his touch didn't mean anything at all. He was just stopping her from falling, that was all. She was the one with the problem.

When he saw that she was all right, he let her go, and she struggled to bring her wayward senses under control. They had a job to do, and she needed all her wits about her so that she could concentrate on the matter in hand.

'Who called it in?' she asked. 'Do you know? First of all, I heard that it was the boy's parents who had rung the emergency services, but then Jack said that wasn't right, and the parents didn't know where he was. He just took off, and they were worried. They were just afraid that something might have happened to him.'

'I understood that the call came from a man who had been out walking his dog. Luckily, the dog had been off his lead, and went nosing about among the outbuildings, otherwise we might never have known the child was here.'

Kayleigh approached the barn. Lewis had stopped to speak to a man who was waiting by the broken-down fence, his dog sitting by his side, and the paramedics were still making their way from the ambulance, bringing with them a stretcher and medical equipment.

She pushed open the creaking door, and went inside, peering through the gloom into the dark corners of the outbuilding. She couldn't fathom why a child would be hiding away in such a dismal place, but she guessed that he must be frightened and unhappy, and that something must have prompted him to run away.

Her heart juddered when she made out the huddled figure of the small boy. He was curled up in a corner, and she realised straight away that he was struggling for air, his breathing fast and shallow, a sheen of sweat on his brow and a dreadful wheezing sound coming from his lungs.

She knelt down beside him. 'Nathan,' she said quietly, 'I'm a doctor. I've come to help you. There's no need for you to be frightened... I just need to listen to your chest and examine you to see how I can make you feel better.'

The boy didn't answer. She guessed that he would find it too difficult to speak in his present condition. He was about seven years old and he was a pitiful sight, thin and pale and clearly in a state of distress.

By now, Lewis had come to join her, and she said softly, 'I've listened to his chest, and I think there may be some infection there. His heart rate is very fast.' The paramedics were already preparing an oxygen mask and nebuliser, and she told the boy, 'We're going to put this mask over your face so that you can breathe in some medicine. It will help to make your chest feel better.'

Lewis was checking the child's blood pressure, and now he said, 'I'll give him a shot of a corticosteroid and a bronchodilator. I think we should add a broad-spectrum antibiotic so that we can deal with any infection. I don't want to wait until we get the results of tests back at the hospital.'

She nodded in agreement, and added in a low voice, 'The sooner we get him back there, the better. I'm worried about the pulse oximeter reading.'

The child was restless, suffering from a lack of oxygen, and it was clear that he was going through a very bad asthma attack. 'Do we know if the parents are on their way to the hospital?'

Tim nodded. 'As soon as the man called it in, we let them know what was happening. I told them that we would be bringing the boy in.'

Hearing that, Nathan tried to speak. 'Mum will be…mad at me,' he managed. His face was taut, his lips pinched. 'Broke…window.'

'I don't think your mum is going to mind any more about the window,' Kayleigh said in a soothing tone. 'She's more worried about you being poorly.'

The boy didn't look so sure about that, and Kayleigh patted his hand in a gesture of sympathy. 'We all do things wrong from time to time,' she said, 'but it doesn't mean that our parents stop loving us.' She glanced at Lewis, expecting him to acknowledge that and put the boy at ease, but she was surprised to see that his expression was somehow closed, his features showing a hint of strain, and there was a sombre tinge of darkness in his eyes that she couldn't fathom.

He seemed to shake off whatever it was that plagued him after a second or two, and he murmured in a light voice, 'We've all done it, lad. I'm sure your mum will know by now that it was an accident.'

He must have convinced the boy, because Nathan appeared to relax a little. 'You think so?'

Lewis nodded. 'I'm sure of it. Your mum loves you. She's been frantic with worry, trying to find you.'

Kayleigh studied Lewis surreptitiously as they prepared to transfer the boy to the ambulance. What had brought about that fleeting grim look to his face? She didn't believe it was the boy's condition that had brought it on, because he had faced much worse cases before this and not shown his concern. This was another matter entirely, she was sure. Was there something in his past that had caused him grief...something that even now had the power to stop him in his tracks? What was it that he wasn't telling her? Did she have any right to ask?

'He seems to be stable for the moment,' Lewis said as they went back to the car, 'but we need to monitor him very carefully as soon as we get back to the hospital. If his condition changes, we may need to intubate him to make sure that he gets sufficient oxygen.'

Kayleigh shared his concerns. They drove back to the Riverside, following the ambulance, and she worried about the boy, but at the same time she was curious about what had affected Lewis's mood back in the barn. She was cautious about questioning him, though.

In many ways, Lewis kept himself to himself. Even though he got on well with all the staff in A and E, and anyone could go to him at any time with any kind of problem, there were moments when he appeared quiet and withdrawn. People respected his privacy, and Kayleigh felt that she ought to do the same. She was new to the department. If no one else had quizzed him about his private life, who was she to step in where others had thought it best to leave well alone?

Even so, she wanted to reach out to him, to touch him and smooth away the crooked line that furrowed his brow.

At the hospital, they followed the child into A and E. This was their last call of the day, and Kayleigh was glad she would be able to stay with the boy and follow his progress.

'We need to make arrangements to admit him to the children's unit,' she told Sharon a while later. 'In the meantime, I want to add ipratropium to his treatment regime. I'm not going off duty just yet—I'd sooner stay around to keep an eye on him for a while longer. Will you let me know when he's about to be transferred?'

'I will.' Sharon checked the boy's monitor. 'I'll give him the nebulised bronchodilator in a few minutes. Hopefully, we should see a change in him after that. His parents will be anxious to know what's happening, so if it's all right with you, I'll go and fetch them and bring them in to see him.'

'Yes, that's good. Just make sure that he stays calm—he was a bit worried that he might be in trouble with them.'

Sharon tucked a wayward strand of chestnut hair behind her ear and smiled. 'I won't let anyone upset him,' she said. 'Though I think his mum and dad are worried out of their minds right now.'

Kayleigh went over to the desk to write up her charts, and just as she was finishing off she glanced over to the waiting room and saw a familiar face. She took a moment to file away the paperwork, and then hurried over to the annexe.

'Jacob,' she said, giving her sister's ex-boyfriend a smile, 'what are you doing here? You haven't done any more damage to yourself, have you?'

He laughed. 'No, thankfully, I managed to stay out of trouble. In fact, I was hoping that I would run into you. I've just been for an X-ray to check that the bones in my arm are healing up in the right way—the fracture clinic people told me to come in for that.'

Kayleigh nodded. 'Have you had the results yet? Is everything as it should be?'

'Yes, I'm doing all right.' He looked at her, his glance thoughtful, his head tilted slightly to one side as though he was weighing her up. 'Do you have time for a cup of coffee? I've been waiting here for so long that I'm a bit parched.'

'Of course. I'm supposed to be off duty anyway. I just want to stay here long enough to check up on a patient. We could fetch a drink from the cafeteria and go and sit outside in the quadrangle, if you like.' She glanced down at the cast on his arm. 'Are you waiting to see the doctor?'

'That's right. They seem to be running late, though. I suppose, if I leave a message with the receptionist, she'll know where to find me, won't she?'

'That's a good idea.'

A few minutes later, they were sitting on the bench outside A and E, taking in the fresh air. 'How have things been for you at work since your accident?' Kayleigh asked. 'It must have been a bitter blow for you, breaking your arm that way. I know how much you liked your job at the leisure centre.'

'The bosses have been fine with me. In fact, they said that I could go back next week and do a desk job until I'm fully healed. They want someone to train the other instructors, so in a way this has been a bit of a boost for me. I can't do the physical stuff, but I can help with the

trainees well enough—showing them the pro-
cedures, how to handle the paperwork, and so
on.'

'I'm glad. I know Heather was really proud
when you passed all your exams and landed
that job.' She was solemn for a while, ponder-
ing events. 'I can't think what went wrong
between you. I know she thought the world of
you.'

His mouth made an odd shape. 'That worked
both ways. I thought she was pretty special...
though you're right, there were problems
towards the end. She suddenly started having
doubts about the two of us and for myself I was
very much aware of the age gap. I know it's
only seven years, but it can make a difference.
We had started to argue a lot. She didn't seem
to be herself, and I wasn't sure what had caused
her to change.'

Kayleigh sighed. 'She was very young, and
perhaps she was confused on several counts. I
wish we could find her again. I just want to talk
to her and persuade her that, whatever was
wrong, we can work things out.'

He laid his hand on hers. 'So do I. It's always

bothered me that things ended on such a sour note, but perhaps Evan was right. Maybe I was the wrong man for her all along. Perhaps I should have paid attention to a girl more my own age…someone like you.' His mouth made a straight line. 'Even so, I didn't expect her to take off like that, and I've always regretted that we didn't get the chance to talk things through properly. I just don't know what more I can do.'

Kayleigh grimaced. 'I've been thinking about that. I've printed out some posters with her picture on them. My boss suggested that I could distribute them throughout the neighbouring counties, in case they might jog someone's memory. If you can think of anyone who would help us to put them out, we might begin to make some headway.'

He looked thoughtful. 'I could take charge of some of that, and I'll ask around to see if I can rope anyone else in. That sounds like a good idea.'

A noise disturbed them, and Kayleigh looked up to see that Lewis had come to join them.

'I wondered if I might find you out here,' he said. 'I hope I'm not interrupting.' He glanced down to where Jacob's hand rested on hers, and Jacob must have believed he had taken it the wrong way, because he carefully broke off the contact.

Kayleigh winced. It was the second time that Lewis had found them holding one another. What must he be thinking?

'You remember Jacob, don't you?' she murmured. 'We were just talking about my sister, and saying how much we both miss her.'

'I can appreciate that.'

Perhaps Jacob saw that Lewis was not convinced about his reasons for being here, and felt he needed to explain. He said cautiously, 'It was me who dragged Kayleigh out here. She said that she was about to go off duty.'

Lewis nodded. 'I saw you both come from the waiting room. I just wanted to let Kayleigh know that the little boy we brought in is beginning to show some signs of improvement...very slight as yet, but at least his blood oxygen level has improved.'

'Has it?' Kayleigh was relieved. 'I'm glad about that. I think that if we can get the infection under control, things should start to look up. I wondered if seeing his parents might help, too, once he realised that they weren't angry with him.'

She glanced at Jacob. 'He was another runaway, but much younger than the teenager who was living in your block of flats. It makes me feel really sad, thinking about these poor children who have taken off from their families. They're young and vulnerable, and it's so much worse when they're ill for any reason.'

Jacob nodded. 'I know how worried you were about Craig. His burn was nasty, but being separated from his family was an extra problem to contend with. In fact, that's one of the reasons I wanted to talk to you.'

'Was it?' She frowned. 'Have you heard some news? The last thing I heard was that he was still in the burns unit receiving treatment. I know his friends have been to see him, and I popped in to see him myself the other day. He seemed a bit depressed.'

'I can imagine he would be. Actually, I was concerned about him myself, and so I started to ask around about him. It occurred to me that he must have been registered at the leisure centre as I've seen him around. All members are given an identity card that shows their photo so that they can take advantage of discounts. I checked our records and came across his photo. I didn't want to take any action myself, but if you want to get in touch with his family, I may be able to help out.'

'That's terrific news.' Kayleigh glanced up at Lewis, trying to gauge his reaction. He hadn't seemed at all concerned about Craig being a runaway, but surely he would agree that they ought to try to reunite the boy with his parents. 'What do you think?' she asked him.

'It wouldn't hurt to make some discreet inquiries,' he murmured. 'I'm just a little wary of putting the boy in touch with his family without knowing the reasons why he left. I don't think he's likely to trust either of us enough to open up, but I would feel happier if we knew what was going on before we made any move.'

'I've spoken to the boy from time to time,' Jacob said. 'We used to come and go from the flats at round about the same time, and quite often we would pass the time of day, or talk about the football, or how he was getting on with his swimming sessions. I wouldn't mind paying a visit to the burns unit and having a chat with him. It's possible that he would confide in me, and I might be able to find out what set this all off.'

'That's brilliant,' Kayleigh said, her mouth curving into a smile. 'Will you let me know what happens?'

'Of course.' He made a crooked grin. 'I've always had a fondness for you, Kayleigh. You know I'll be glad to help you in any way I can.'

He got to his feet. 'I should go now…I expect the doctor will be ready to see me soon. I'll be in touch.' He gave her a hug, using his good arm to embrace her, and then started towards the building.

Kayleigh watched him go. She hoped something would come of his chat with the boy. Lewis may not be concerned about the family getting back together, but she was.

'You and Jacob seem to get on very well together,' Lewis said, as they walked back into A and E a moment later. 'I know you said he was your sister's boyfriend, but he seems to be very taken with you.'

Her eyes widened. 'Does he? Well, we've always been great friends.'

'I think it's more than that. He has a way of looking at you...and there's definitely a closeness between you.'

Kayleigh acknowledged that with a nod. 'He's a good man. My stepfather may not have liked him, but I think he was wrong in his judgment. Jacob has always worked hard, and I know he's a man that you could rely on.' She was quiet for a moment, and then she added, 'If anyone can find out what's going on with that young teenage boy, he'll be the one to do it.'

Lewis didn't press the point, but she guessed that he was weighing up the situation. It probably wouldn't do any harm to let him think that she might be involved in some way with Jacob. After the way Lewis had kissed her the other day, she needed some form of defence.

The truth was, she didn't want to let her guard down around any man. It seemed that Lewis had his own hang-up about her background, and over the years she had learned to be wary, because her family's relative wealth had been an issue with a lot of the men she had dated. Either they had been intrigued by her background or they had wanted to take control, as if to show that it didn't matter, that they were superior, with or without money. But with Lewis it seemed to be a combination of her family and how close they were, as well as possibly her wealth. It was a bad situation all round, because her material status really didn't matter to her. What mattered was that the people in her life were there for her, and she for them…but she had to acknowledge that nothing had worked out quite the way she wanted.

She went to check up on Nathan, and was pleased to see that his breathing seemed a little easier. Even so, he looked small and frail in the big bed, and she wanted to scoop him up in her arms and cuddle him. As she watched over him, the paediatrician came to supervise his transfer to the children's unit, and Kayleigh saw him off, hoping desperately that all would go well for him.

'You look as though he touched a nerve with you,' Lewis said, coming up behind her. 'Do you have a soft spot for our little patient?'

Startled out of her reverie, Kayleigh turned to look at him. She nodded. 'I hate to see children looking so poorly. With him, somehow, the feeling was stronger. I wanted to pick him up and cuddle him, but, of course, I can't do that.'

'No, you can't.' An odd, strangely bleak expression crossed his face, and she realised that she had absolutely no idea what he was thinking.

She said cautiously, 'I suppose you think it's wrong of me to feel that way…kind of unprofessional?'

'Children can have that effect on you, but it's not our place to stand in for their mothers. There's a cut-off point where you need to stand back.'

'I know…but it's hard to do that.' She looked at him. 'Well, it is for me, anyway.' Perhaps it wasn't difficult for him at all.

He didn't answer, and she guessed he had put up the barriers to any exchange of ideas on that point. His face had a closed look about it, and he turned away to deal with his lab test forms.

Kayleigh went to hand over her patients to the next shift, and then went over to the children's unit to take a last look at Nathan. He was sleeping, and his blood oxygen level was creeping up, bit by bit. Satisfied, she left the hospital and went home to see how Aunt Jane was coping.

'She's not had a very good day,' Margaret told her. She looked concerned, her blue eyes troubled, her wavy black hair awry. 'I had to call out the GP, and he came and gave her something to settle her down. He said her heart rate was chaotic, with some sort of rhythm disturbance, he said—but whatever he gave her seems to have helped. If it hadn't, he was going to send her to the hospital. I didn't want to call you at work, especially as the treatment seemed to help. She's resting now.'

'Thanks, Margaret. I'm sorry you had to deal with that. I don't know how I would manage without you. You've been wonderful.'

'I'm glad to do it. You know, I've always thought of Jane as a good friend, one of the best. I hate to see her this way.'

'We all do.' Kayleigh saw Margaret out of the door, and then went to check on her aunt.

She was still sleeping, and she looked peaceful so Kayleigh didn't disturb her. It was worrying that she'd had such a bad time, and it bothered her that they hadn't yet got to the bottom of what was causing the trouble.

She went into the kitchen to prepare supper,

and as she looked out of the window she saw that Lewis was in the garden. He was forking over the flower-beds, pulling up weeds and generally tidying things up.

Kayleigh went out to him. 'I thought you might like a cup of tea,' she said, placing a mug down on a low stone wall. She looked at his handiwork. 'You know, you don't have to do any of this. I'm getting round to it, little by little.'

He straightened up, and looked her over. 'I know, but I told your aunt that I would do it in return for the bits and pieces that she's been giving me. It's no bother, and it keeps me fit in the process.'

Kayleigh studied his lithe form. That was true enough. He had changed into casual clothes, but it was plain to see that his body was toned to perfection. His muscles were taut, his biceps straining against the short sleeves of the T-shirt he was wearing and his blue denims moulded his strong legs.

She looked away. He was too much to take in right now, and she didn't want to be held to ransom by her own wayward senses. He was just a man, like any other man, and she ought to remember that. None of them were to be trusted.

'Even so,' she said, 'there's a lot to do, and it isn't your responsibility, though I do appreciate you helping out. I try to do a bit on my days off. Perhaps I could give you a hand with your decorating in return.'

He glanced at her. 'Thanks. It would certainly get things done a lot quicker with two people working on it.' He took a moment to lean his forearm on the garden fork. 'Your mother must have appreciated the garden,' he said. 'There's a lot of land here, and it's been well designed. There are all sorts of different areas to the garden, lots of nooks and crannies and places of interest.'

'She did, but Heather was the one who loved the garden most of all. She planted out a lot of the flower-beds and she organised the decking. We had a gardener to do most of the work, but Heather liked to potter, and my aunt used to be out here almost every day. I suppose that's why we let the gardener go. Heather said that she could manage.'

She gazed around, her glance trailing over the pond. 'The water irises are beautiful this time of year—they were Heather's favourites. I remember my mother looking at them in the month or so before she died. She must have been thinking about Heather. It broke her heart when she didn't come back.'

'She wrote, though, didn't she?' Lewis was frowning. 'Your aunt said that there was a postcard. That must have given your mother some comfort.'

Kayleigh nodded. 'Yes, that's right. It was just so sad that she didn't ever come back. Perhaps, if we had been able to get in touch with her, we could have let her know that Evan had gone.'

Lewis was thoughtful. 'Did she never get in touch with Jacob?'

'No, she didn't. She ended their relationship very suddenly, and then she just took off. It was very strange, because they had been very close, and I even thought they might marry at some stage.'

'Didn't you have any idea that she was planning to go?'

Kayleigh shook her head. 'No... She had been

a bit off colour, and we thought that she had gone to her room to lie down. She had that terrible row with Evan, so bad that I heard her being sick just a short time later. She said she felt a bit faint, and I helped her up to her room and made sure that she was comfortable.'

Her eyes misted over with tears. 'She lay down on the bed, and said, "You know you're my best friend, don't you? I think the world of you, and Mum, and Aunt Jane." I didn't realise it then, but she was saying goodbye.'

Lewis came and put his arms around her, and for a little while she felt as though she had found a safe place where she could leave her troubles behind. She rested her head on his chest and felt the steady thud of his heartbeat beneath her cheek. He smelt of fresh air and grass, and of something essentially male, something that stirred her senses and made her want to stay there, locked in his arms for a long, long time.

He said softly, 'We'll do whatever we can to find her. I'll help you. I'm sure she must be out there somewhere, waiting for you to bring her back.'

She looked up at him. He was being kind to her, doing what he could to soothe her troubles away, and she was grateful to him for that. It didn't mean anything, the way that he was holding her... He was just showing her that he cared, and that she wasn't on her own, just as he would for anyone who needed comfort.

'Thank you for that. It makes me feel better, knowing that I'm not alone in this.' She straightened up and eased herself away from him a little.

He said cautiously, 'You said that your sister broke things off with Jacob—that she was upset, and feeling off colour. Has it occurred to you that there might have been another reason for her to be feeling faint and sick? It might not have been just the argument with your stepfather that brought matters to a head, but perhaps Jacob played a big part in that, too. There could have been a particular reason for her to take off the way she did.'

Kayleigh stared at him, the full import of what he was saying beginning to dawn on her. 'You're saying...the sickness and the fainting were symptoms...' She broke off, trying to take it in. 'You think she might have been pregnant?'

He nodded. 'Isn't that a possibility?'

Her mouth dropped open in shock, and then she quickly clamped it shut. Recovering, she said, 'Yes…I mean, no…I don't know. Perhaps you could be right. I hadn't thought of that before now.'

She gazed at him, her grey eyes clouded. 'What am I going to do? I have to find her…now, more than ever. I shan't rest until I know that she's safe.'

He put up a hand and cupped her cheek with his palm, his thumb brushing away a stray tear that trickled down her face. 'You don't have to carry this burden on your own, Kayleigh, but it's something that you need to come to terms with, otherwise the fallout is going to colour the rest of your life. I've seen the way you are at work— you get emotional and over-involved with the patients, and that probably has something to do with all that's going on in your home life. It can't be good for you to be under such a nervous strain, especially in the kind of work we do. Try not to worry about what's going on. I told you…I'll help you through this, in any way I can.'

She tried a smile, but it was a vestige of the

real thing. He was holding her close and offering her support, and she felt as though she was being drawn into a cocoon of warmth, a place of refuge.

Even so, she shouldn't read anything personal into that. He thought her problems were affecting her work, and that was why he was taking more than a passing interest in her private life. It wasn't because she was special to him, or because he cared about her any more than was usual. She needed to keep up her guard, and not allow herself to fall for him. That path was strewn with pitfalls.

CHAPTER SIX

'WE'VE made some headway in the last hour or
so, haven't we?' Kayleigh put down her paint-
brush and took a look around the dining room,
her gaze absorbing the soft buttermilk colour of
the walls and the clean lines of the white glossed
window frames.

'We certainly have,' Lewis said, on a note of
satisfaction. 'I didn't think we would get this far
this afternoon, but with your help we've made
fast work of it.'

'I imagine your friend will be pleased to come
back to see all this.' She wiped her hands on a
damp cloth. 'Do you think you'll miss it when
you leave? After all, it's taken quite a lot of hard
work to get this far, and you might not get to appreciate it for very long once he comes home.'

Lewis nodded. 'I'm sure he'll be very happy

with what we've done. He hadn't long moved into this place and he knew that a lot needed doing to it to put things right. Anyway, I doubt that I will be leaving straight away when he gets back. He offered me a room for as long as I need it.'

'Did he?' She lifted a brow at that. 'It sounds as though you and he get along very well.'

'Yes, we do. We were at school together, so we go back a long way.'

She smiled. 'It's good to have friends like that.' She still didn't quite understand why he wasn't looking for a place of his own. As a consultant, she would have imagined he would value his independence and want to make his standard of living more secure and organised, but perhaps he preferred to lodge with a friend. At least they would be company for each other. In any event, she didn't feel that she was ready to ask him. He could be remote at times, keeping things to himself, and he might take it the wrong way if she started to probe. She didn't want to find herself shut off from him now that they were getting on well together.

Distracted, Kayleigh studied the pots of emulsion paint that stood on a nearby table. The surface was covered with layers of newspaper, which was just as well, considering that there were drips of paint all around from brushes and minor accidents.

'It looks as though you're about out of both colours,' she said, 'and you still have to work on the bedroom, don't you? There might be some more tins in the shed. Shall we go and have a look?'

'That sounds like a good idea. Just give me a minute to clean up, and I'll come with you.'

Kayleigh went to the bathroom to wash her hands, and after a few minutes she came back to find that Lewis was ready. He must have washed up in the kitchen, because by now he, too, was free of paint smears.

'After you,' he said, resting his hand lightly on the small of her back as they went through the doorway.

She registered his touch with a small intake of breath. The warmth from his palm permeated her thin cotton top and sent little sparks of sensation shooting along her spine to stimulate every nerve ending in her body. She didn't want to feel this way, and she didn't understand at all why he should have this effect on her. It put her at a disadvantage, and made her aware of him in a way that sent the blood rushing to her head. It was more than she could cope with right now.

'It's just as well that you didn't repair the gap in the fence,' he said laughingly as they went outside. 'That would have cut off my footpath into the garden. Have you thought about having a gate put in there instead?'

'Well, that would be something to consider, wouldn't it? I suppose it would depend on how neighbourly we want to be. Is your friend likely to want to come and pay us a visit whenever he feels like it?'

He nodded, his blue eyes glinting. 'When he sees the gorgeous girl who lives next door, I'd say that was a distinct possibility.'

'And I bet you say that to all the girls.' Even so, her cheeks flushed warmly at the compliment. Did he really think she was gorgeous?

His mouth curved in a smile. 'In the meantime, it gives me the ideal opportunity to come and rummage without disturbing you or your aunt. Besides, it gives me access to all the gardening tools, so that I can keep your garden and mine up to scratch. Jane said she was OK with that.'

'I know she is. Do you want to go and search for the paint on the far shelves?' Kayleigh said as they reached the shed. 'I don't think I want to climb over all the rubbish that's in the way. Perhaps I'll make a start on clearing some of it.'

He looked around. 'That's probably a good idea,' he murmured. 'What is all that junk, anyway?'

Kayleigh glanced around. 'It's just some of the stuff we cleared out from the house when we had the decorators in.' There was an old cupboard that was being used for storing lengths of cable and batteries and so on, along with spare parts for some of the domestic equipment. Then there were boxes filled with bits and pieces that they were undecided about but couldn't quite bring themselves to throw away.

In front of the shelving, she discovered a small wooden box, discoloured with age now, but she remembered that it belonged to Heather. It used to hold a porcelain doll, and as far as she could recall the porcelain doll was on a chair in Heather's room.

'There's some silk emulsion here,' Lewis said. 'It says "Honeydew" on the label—do you think it would be all right for me to use that? The tin seems to be fairly full.'

Kayleigh nodded. 'Yes, that would be fine.' She unfastened the metal clasp on the box and carefully opened the lid.

'Are you OK?' Lewis asked. 'You've gone very quiet all of a sudden.'

She glanced up at him. 'These are some of Heather's things—old postcards, mostly. I expect she was thinking of throwing them out.' She riffled through them, and then picked one out, gazing down at it.

Lewis came to stand by her side, looking at the card over her shoulder. 'I think I know that bay—isn't it known as a popular surfing beach, just along the coast?'

'That's right. We used to go there at least once every summer. Heather thought it was pretty spectacular. She liked looking at the waves coming in, and we would go for walks along the clifftop sometimes. I think it was one of her favourite places.'

Lewis draped an arm around her, laying a

hand on her shoulder. It was just a casual gesture as he moved in to take a closer look at the picture, but Kayleigh found her senses stirring, thrown into chaos by his nearness. She could feel the warmth of his skin as his face bent close to hers, and for a moment she felt as though she had stopped breathing, as though the world had stood still.

'Maybe we should make that our first port of call,' he said.

She turned to look at him. 'What do you mean?'

'We could take a drive over there, and put up some of the posters in the shops round about, or hand them out to people and ask them to enquire among their friends as to whether they've seen her.'

Kayleigh nodded. 'Yes...that would be as good a place as any to start. It won't take us too long to get there, will it?'

'About an hour, I'd say. Maybe we could go straight after work tomorrow? We both finish early, don't we? We've half a day out with the ambulance, and then we're both off for the afternoon. It was supposed to be my day in the lecture hall, but they've closed it down temporarily for repairs to the ceiling, which means that you won't be attending the lecture either. What do you think?'

'I'd like that. I'll feel better once I know I'm doing something positive to find her.'

'That's settled, then.' He glanced down at the paint pot in his hand. 'I'll go and make a make a start on the bedroom. Are you coming back over to the house with me?'

She thought about that. 'I'd better not. I ought to go and check up on my aunt, and keep her company.' Anyway, it would be better for her to distance herself from him for a while. Her pulses were still racing, and even in the unlikely setting of this old wooden shed, she was finding his nearness too much to handle.

Over the last few weeks, she had come to realise that it would be all too easy to grow close to him, but all her instincts warned her that she could end up hurt. No relationships were without their problems. Her mother had come to realise that she had made a mistake in her marriage to Evan, and it seemed that her sister had had second thoughts about Jacob. Why should it be any different for her? She had gone down this road before and discovered that it led to disappointment and disillusionment, and she wasn't ready to trust her heart to any one.

'I'll see you at work tomorrow, then,' he said.

'All right.'

The time passed quickly enough, and she met up with him at the ambulance station early the next day. There was little time for chitchat, though. The whole morning was taken up with emergency callouts—first a road traffic accident, and then they went out to a man who had managed to trap his arm in some machinery at his place of work. They dealt with each case successfully, but on their final trip out Kayleigh could see from the outset that this latest rescue mission was going to be difficult, as well as traumatic.

A little girl had taken a tumble over the side of a cliff, and as yet no one knew the full extent of her injuries. Her parents were totally stressed out, and it was taking everything Jack had to calm them down.

'I think perhaps you should stay here, by the ambulance,' Lewis said, glancing at Kayleigh. They were standing on the clifftop overlooking the sea, and though there was a stretch of sandy beach some distance below them, the tide was steadily coming in. 'I'll try to work my way down the cliffside to see if I can reach the little girl. She seems to have come to rest on an overhang. It doesn't look too safe, and the sandstone is crumbling—I don't think it would be wise for you to attempt to go down there.'

'I'm not going to just stand here and wait while that little girl suffers,' Kayleigh said. 'Tim is going to need help getting the stretcher down there, and you don't have any idea how badly the child is hurt. You might not be able to manage on your own.'

He shook his head. 'I'm responsible for you and I won't put you in any kind of danger.'

'I'm responsible for myself,' she retorted. 'Besides, I've had some practice with abseiling. I think I can get myself down there and be of some use…just as long as we have the right equipment to hand. The lines need to be fastened securely at the top of the cliff.'

Lewis nodded. 'The coastguard are seeing to all that.' He frowned. 'Are you sure that you want to do this?'

'I'm sure.' Kayleigh's jaw was firm. 'The coastguard aren't medically trained, and even from this distance I can see that the girl is in a bad way. Let's not waste any more time debating the issue. We need to get down there.'

Lewis started to ease himself into his harness. 'I'll go first and make sure that we have secure footholds. I don't want you to take any risks at all,' he said. 'Make sure that you follow my signal.'

She acknowledged that with a curt nod. As long as the line held fast, she was confident that she could do this. What was worrying was the fact that the ledge the child was lying on was liable to give way at any time. She hadn't missed the notices posted along the clifftop, warning of danger, and this was the very last mission she would have hoped for.

Carefully, she followed Lewis's lead and began to edge her way down the cliffside, searching for footholds with the toe of her shoe. She used her hands to steady herself from time to time and a clump of earth came away in her fingers and skittered down onto the beach below. A film of sweat broke out on her brow.

Looking down, she could see that the little

girl wasn't moving, and when they came level with her Kayleigh said softly, 'Lucy...can you hear me? Can you tell me what happened to you?'

The child mumbled something, and Kayleigh tried again. 'Can you tell me your name?'

'Lucy...Simmons,' the girl's voice faded.

'How old are you, Lucy?' Kayleigh knew that the child was six years old, but she wanted to see whether she was capable of responding in a logical manner. The little girl didn't answer.

'It looks as though she has a head injury,' Lewis said, his voice taking on a grim note. 'We'll have to get the harness tied around her, but we must make sure that we keep her head and spine stable, just in case there's a neck injury along with everything else.'

As he spoke, Tim was making his way down the cliffside with one of the coastguard. They were lowering with them a contraption that looked like a metal cage.

Kayleigh was busy checking the girl's pulse and blood pressure, and as she did so, the child started to vomit. 'Don't worry about that,' she said quietly. She helped Lewis to roll the girl gently onto her side to prevent her from choking. 'You've hurt your head, Lucy, that's why you're feeling sick.'

When the sickness bout was over, Lewis carefully put a collar around the girl's neck, while Kayleigh worked to obtain intravenous access.

'It looks as though her skull is fractured,' Lewis said. 'There are bone fragments pressing downwards onto the brain surface, and she's losing blood. I'm going to put a sterile gauze dressing over the wound, but we need to get some fluids into her.'

Kayleigh agreed. She worked efficiently to set up the fluid line and continued to try to get the child to talk, but it was becoming clear that Lucy's condition was deteriorating and the girl was slipping into unconsciousness. 'Her pulse rate is falling, and her blood pressure is rising. We have to get her to hospital as soon as possible.' She put an oxygen mask in place over her face to help the child to breathe.

A moment or so later, Lucy started to convulse, and Kayleigh's face paled as the ledge she was resting on began to give way under the extra pressure.

Lewis acted swiftly. He had hold of the girl's harness, but now he clipped it to his waistband as a precaution, and tried to steady her. He used all his strength to keep the line that was holding him from swaying, holding onto a grassy outcrop to try to keep himself still.

Kayleigh had been thrown sideways as part of the overhang that she was kneeling on crumbled away, and now she was struggling to regain her balance. She toppled, and the momentum sent her crashing against the side of the cliff, so that she grazed her forehead on the rough, craggy surface.

'Are you all right?' Lewis said, shooting her a searching look.

'I'm fine,' Kayleigh murmured. 'How is Lucy doing?'

'She's not too good.'

'Do you think we can get her into the wire cradle?' Tim said. 'I have it secured at my end. Once we get her safely in there, you can unclip her from your harness and the coast-guard can winch her up from the clifftop while we steady her.'

'Yes, we'll do that. Just let me have a moment so that I can give her an anticonvulsant first.'

Lewis was grim-faced, working as fast as he was able. He was clearly worried about this little girl.

It was a few minutes before they managed to bring her up to the top of the cliff. Lucy's parents were distraught, but Lewis concentrated his attention on his patient.

'I'm going to intubate her,' he said, once they had released her from the wire cradle that had held her safe. 'She's not going to be able to breathe properly unless I do that.'

As soon as he had the tube in place, and the paramedic came and took over with the supply of oxygen, Lewis signalled that she could be taken into the ambulance. 'I'll ring ahead to warn the neurologist that we're on our way. She'll need a CT scan, so that we can assess the damage.'

He turned to the parents. 'Lucy has a nasty head injury, but we're not sure yet as to the extent of her injuries. Once we get her back to the hospital, we can assess her condition more accurately. In the meantime, we're doing everything we can to stabilise her. If you want to follow the ambulance, you'll be able to see her as soon as we get her to A and E.'

'Thank you, Doctor,' the child's mother said

in a choked voice. 'I know that you've all done everything that you possibly can for her. Thank you so much for helping her.'

Lewis nodded. He turned towards the fast-response car, and Kayleigh finished gathering together all of the medical equipment and then hurried after him.

'She's not doing too well at all, is she?'

He shook his head. 'No, she isn't. I'm glad this is the last call of the morning. I want to stay with her and see this one through.'

'Me, too,' Kayleigh murmured.

Back at the hospital, Lucy was rushed to X-Ray for a CT scan. Lewis and Kayleigh went along with her.

'I don't like the way things are going,' Lewis said. 'She's going downhill too fast. The intra-cranial pressure is rising. Where's the neurologist? I expected him to be here by now, but there's no sign of him.'

The nurse intervened at that. 'I put out a call for him, but he's operating and can't get away. I asked for a member of his team, but they're all working on emergencies.'

'You told him this was urgent?'

'Yes, of course.'

'Ring him again. Tell him we need him down here now.'

Sharon hurried away to make the call, and Lewis turned back to the CT images that were flashing up on the computer monitor. 'There it is…do you see it?' he said, glancing at Kayleigh.

She pulled in a quick breath. 'A haematoma…yes, I see it. That's a huge blood clot—we have to do something quickly.'

'You're right.' He turned as Sharon came towards them, shaking her head.

'He's going to be at least another half-hour.'

'We can't wait that long—I'm going to have to evacuate the clot right now. We need to set up for the procedure…'

They all hurried to prepare the child for surgery and a few minutes later Kayleigh watched, her whole body tense, as Lewis worked to remove the clot that was pressing dangerously on the child's brain tissues. His expression was grim, but his concentration never failed, and she realised that she had every confidence in him. He was a dedicated doctor with a sure touch, and if anyone could save this child, he would.

'I'll use diathermy to seal the blood vessel,' he said, getting ready to finish off. 'Is there any sign of the neurosurgeon yet?'

'He's on his way,' Sharon told him.

'About time...'

They watched Lucy's transfer to the neurology team, and then went to clean up. Lewis glanced at his watch. 'The day hasn't gone quite as we expected, and we're running late, but we've still time to drive over to the surfers' bay.' He glanced at Kayleigh. 'Are you still up for it?'

She nodded. 'There's no point in waiting around here—we won't know how Lucy's going to hold up for some time. It's all in the hands of the medical team now.'

'That's true. I'll check up on her later on today.' He started to head towards the locker room. 'I suggest we start out for the coast right away. Perhaps we'll get some lunch when we get to the bay, unless you're hungry now?'

'That will be fine. After all the drama this morning, I think I need to let my stomach settle.'

She went to change into her casual clothes, a sleeveless top and filmy cotton skirt, and met up with him by the reception desk just a short time later.

'Someone was looking for you,' the clerk said, glancing from one to the other. 'I knew that you were with a patient, and I was just coming to see if I could find you.'

'Someone was looking for both of us?' Kayleigh asked.

The girl nodded. 'He's over there, waiting to see the doctor for a follow-up appointment. His name's Craig. Apparently he was recently discharged from the burns unit.'

Kayleigh glanced through to the waiting room. 'It's the boy from the block of flats,' she said to Lewis. 'Do you remember him?'

'Of course. We were worried that he had run away from home.'

They thanked the clerk for passing on the message, and then they both started towards the boy.

'Hello, Craig,' Kayleigh said. 'How are you? Does the arm feel any easier now?'

Craig nodded. 'They say I have to keep the dressing on for a while yet, and I have to keep coming back to Outpatients so that they can see how I'm doing.' He hesitated, looking a little awkward. 'I wanted to say that I'm sorry for giving you a hard time over my parents, and so on. It's just that I was worried that I would be in trouble—I haven't been getting on all that well with my mum's boyfriend, and I was cheeky to him and did some things I shouldn't have done. Then I realised I'd gone too far and I thought maybe it would be better if I left.'

He grimaced. 'I didn't think anyone wouldn't miss me, but one of the men who lives in the same block of flats as my friend came and talked to me. He sorted things out between my mum and me, and I realised that she'd been really upset.'

'So have you gone back to live with your mum now?' Lewis asked.

'Yes. We're getting on much better than we did before…and I've told her that I'll try and get along with Tony, her boyfriend. We seem to have just misunderstood each other.' He pressed his lips together. 'I'm sorry that I was so diffi-cult. I know that you were only trying to help.'

Lewis made a faint smile. 'We can all be dif-ficult from time to time, especially when everything seems to be against us. I'm glad things have worked out all right for you.'

'That goes for me, too,' Kayleigh said.

As they said goodbye to the boy and walked away a few moments later, she cast a surreptitious glance in Lewis's direction. There was a glimmer of satisfaction in his eyes, and she was pleased about that. Perhaps he wasn't as tough as he made out. He did his best to appear not to care that families might be torn apart by their differences, but it was quite clear that he was glad that this one had managed to sort their problems out. Maybe there was a chink in his armour after all.

They drove down to the beach that had been among Heather's favourites, and stopped to hand out posters to passers-by and drop them into shops where the owners agreed to let them put them up on display.

'We haven't had much luck up to now,' Kayleigh said with a frown after they had been doing this for some half-hour or so. 'No one seems to have seen her.' She was dismayed by their lack of success. Perhaps she had made the mistake of pinning too much hope on this venture.

'These are early days yet,' Lewis murmured. 'People have been helpful and we've been able to put up the posters in lots of places along the seafront and down the side streets. It might take a week or so before we can expect any result.' He sent her a quick glance. 'I think perhaps we've done all we can for today, and we should stop and go and get something to eat now. That might make both of us feel better.'

Kayleigh was happy to agree to that. They had lunch in a restaurant that had a balcony terrace overlooking the sea, and as they ate they were able to take in the magnificent view of the bay.

Kayleigh chose a salad, while Lewis tucked into a lasagne. Neither of them said very much, simply relaxing for a while and absorbing the fresh sea air.

The tide was going out, and waves broke on the shore in white, foamy rivulets. The golden sweep of beach was smooth, except where children ran and dipped their toes into the water, leaving small footprints in the sand.

'This is a beautiful place,' Kayleigh murmured, finishing off her dessert, a chilled dish of fresh fruit served with a topping of ice cream. 'It's so peaceful. I could sit here and watch the sea for hours. Couldn't you?'

He nodded. 'I know what you mean. It's a fantastic view, with the wide stretch of sand and the blue ocean, and the cliffs in the distance.'

They drank their coffee and left the restaurant a few minutes later, making their way down to the seafront.

'I could see myself living somewhere like this,' Kayleigh murmured as they made their way back to the car. 'Can you imagine getting up each morning and looking out at the bay? When the sun shines down on the water it looks as though it's made up of shimmering jewels.'

'I can imagine it, but you see some of that from where you live now, don't you?'

'Yes, but the house is old and set back a way, and the cobbled streets are narrow and winding down to the cove. I have a lot of good memories of the house, but I'm beginning to think that I'd much rather live somewhere more modern.'

They walked through a landscaped rose garden that led towards the car park. There were high-sided privet hedges along the way, trimmed to form archways and secluded corners. She turned to him. 'Do you remember the house we passed on the journey down here? I pointed it out to you when we turned on to the coast road.'

'The barn conversion? That wasn't far from where we live now.'

'I know.' Her mouth made a fleeting curve. 'I've been to see it at close quarters, and it's glorious. The builder is still working on it, and it's going to be magnificent when it's finally done. The area all around is relatively flat and rural, but it's set back from the clifftop on the curve of the bay so that you can see for miles around, and there's a gentle slope down to the sea. I love it. I think Aunt Jane would like it, too.'

He smiled down at her absorbed expression. 'It's obviously made an impression on you. I don't think I've ever seen you look so enchanted with something.'

'Yes, well…it is a dream house…my fantasy house, anyway.' She laughed, gazing up at him. There was no way she was going to achieve her dream any time soon, but there was no law against indulging in a flight of fancy, was there?

The sun was shining down on her, warming her bare shoulders, and she breathed in air that was fragrant with the scent of roses. She would have put up a hand to shield her eyes from the burning rays, but Lewis moved in closer to her, and in the next moment he had taken her in his arms and he was kissing her, his mouth brushing hers with a gossamer touch, sending waves of pleasure to race along her bloodstream.

Her heart started to hammer, thudding heavily against her rib cage, and as he deepened the kiss, she was conscious that his heart was pounding, too, setting up a wild, erratic rhythm. She felt the heat of his embrace as his hands stroked the length of her arms, and then the gentle pressure of his palm on the small of her back as he drew her towards him, so that the softness of her breasts was crushed against his hard chest.

She had no idea what might have happened next, but the sound of voices reached them, coming from the other side of the hedge, and Lewis reluctantly let her go. They moved a little apart from one another, and she stood for a moment, bewildered, her mind stumbling dazedly through a cloud of cotton wool.

She looked up at him, still hazy from what had happened between them, and he gave her a quizzical, unfathomable look in return. 'I don't know what made me do that,' he said, 'except that you looked so sweet and feminine, and utterly kissable.'

'Oh,' she said. She blinked, trying to take that in.

He gave a soft laugh and laid a hand lightly on her arm, leading her through the archway towards the car park.

'You were telling me about the house,' he said. 'I would have thought it was well within your means to buy it.'

'I suppose so.' She was glad of the change of conversation. It meant that she didn't have to think too deeply, and that was just as well, because her mind had dissolved into marshmallow the instant his arms had closed around her.

They reached the car, and when he opened the door for her, she slid into the passenger seat.

He started up the engine. 'If you like the house that much, why don't you put in an offer to buy it? I take it that eventually it's going to be put up for sale?'

She made a doubtful murmur. 'I'm not sure about that. I heard that someone bought the dilapidated barn and had an architect design the renovation. I don't know whether they're planning to move in at some point or whether it was bought as an investment. Anyway, I can't put in an offer for it. I have to keep the family home open in case Heather comes back. How would she find us if we were to move away? It's her one point of reference.'

'And what will you do if she never comes back?' he asked softly. 'We're doing all that we can, but you have to accept that you might not ever find her. How will you cope with that? Are you going to put the rest of your life on hold?'

'If it comes to that, I suppose that's what I would do.' She gazed at him steadily. 'I told you that the house was only a dream, a castle in the air.'

He shook his head and she could see that he thought she was setting herself up for heartache. She said quietly, 'Where would you live, if you could choose?'

He shrugged. 'It doesn't matter to me, as long as it was somewhere reasonably close to the hospital. For me, a house is just a place to stay, a roof over my head.'

'I think you're wrong. It's more than that…a lot more…but I suppose from my point of view it's the people who live there that make a house into a home. Do you ever think about having a family of your own one day?'

He made a grimace. 'I wouldn't say it features high on my list. I really don't share your love of family.'

She studied him for a moment, trying to work out what it was that made him tick. He was a man full of contradictions. 'You've only ever talked about your father,' she murmured. 'You said that he was ill, but he didn't like to be fussed over. Was that difficult for you? You were very young after all.'

'It wasn't difficult. I learned to understand that he was who he was…a man who didn't tolerate weakness in himself or in those around him. He always thought he knew best, and he wanted things done his way. There wasn't usually any discussion to be had.'

'You sound as though you didn't always agree with him.'

'No, I didn't.' His jaw lifted, and for a moment he stared out into space, looking blankly at the road ahead. 'He wanted me to follow in his footsteps and go to work in the family business, CC Technologies. It had grown into an international company, providing electronic systems, and I would have worked my way up from the basics until eventually I might have handled the overseas branch.'

Kayleigh frowned. 'But you didn't do that…'

'No. I wanted to study medicine. That was all I had wanted to do since I was about twelve years old.'

'How did your father take it when you told him?'

His mouth made a wry shape. 'Let's just say that he didn't take it well.'

'But now that you've reached the top of your profession—you're a consultant, you're respected and people look up to you. What does he feel about it now?'

His shoulders lifted. 'I've no idea. You have to appreciate that I haven't spoken to my father in a long while.'

'Surely he must be proud of you?' She

couldn't imagine a man not being pleased with his son's achievements. 'Hasn't he tried to talk to you about it?'

His brows drew together in a straight line. 'You have to understand how my father thinks about things. Money means everything to him, and he uses it as a bargaining counter. He's a wealthy man, but he threatened to cut me off from my inheritance if I didn't do as he wanted, and he fully expected me to cave in to his demands. I didn't. I refused to do that. So he went ahead and cut me off. He said I had let him down and he would no longer acknowledge me.'

Kayleigh opened her mouth to say something and then shut it again. She couldn't believe that previously she had thought he might have resented her privileged background. Now she understood it was how close she was to her family that was the most marked difference in their childhoods. How could anyone do that to his own son? She said slowly, 'How did you feel about that? Did you try to reason with him…perhaps later, when you first qualified as a doctor?'

He manoeuvred the car up to a junction and then turned on to the coast road. 'No, I didn't do that. The money wasn't important to me, and once he had made the decision to cut me out of his life, I accepted it and moved on. There's no point in raking over the ashes. What's done is done.'

'Surely your mother must have had something to say about it? Didn't she try to make him change his mind?'

His eyes darkened and she saw that his jaw had suddenly clenched. 'I don't want to talk about my mother.'

'I'm sorry.' She didn't know how to take what he had told her. His world must have fallen apart when his father had broken off all ties with him, and it was ironic to think that now he was staying in a friend's house, when he could have had the world at his feet. He still could, in a way, because after all he was at the pinnacle of his career, and he could pick and choose, but whatever had happened with his family must have left a disastrous mark on him.

She said cautiously, 'That must have been very hurtful for you, being cast out by the people who should love you and care about you. I don't know how I would have coped under such circumstances.'

He sent her a swift, quelling look. 'I don't need your sympathy, Kayleigh, so don't waste your breath giving it. I'm not like you, and I don't feel the need to have family around me, as you do. Let's leave it at that, shall we?'

She was stung by his curt dismissal, but perhaps it was no wonder that he had a chip on his shoulder. Was he put out because he had let his guard down and told her more than he wanted to? Or was he really as tough and independent as he appeared?

She winced. The trouble was, she suspected that he was right. He didn't need anyone, least of all her.

CHAPTER SEVEN

KAYLEIGH pressed her fingertips against a knot of tension that was driving its way into her forehead. She was having trouble getting into the day, but perhaps she would feel better with some caffeine inside her.

She went over to the coffee-machine that was set up on a table in a small, enclosed bay off the main corridor and helped herself to a cup, taking a reviving sip of the hot, dark liquid.

'You look as though you have something on your mind,' Lewis said, appearing and coming to stand beside her. 'Are you having problems with one of your cases?'

'One of my cases?' She swivelled around in order to look at him properly, and then added, 'No, no...it's nothing like that.' He was long and lean and dressed in immaculate dark trousers and a pristine shirt in a shade of blue that matched his eyes. He was heart-meltingly attractive.

She pressed her lips together, disturbed by the way he managed to upset her peace of mind. Wasn't he the source of a lot of her troubles? Why was she so aware of a man who could distance himself from love and family feeling and keep himself detached from a good part of what made for normal human emotions?

He lifted a dark brow, watching her steadily. 'I know something is bothering you,' he said softly. 'I recognise the look. You have that far-away, distracted gaze that I've seen before whenever you have something on your mind. If it's not a patient, then it must be something else. Don't you want to talk about it?'

She gave a small sigh. 'I suppose I'm worrying about my aunt,' she admitted. 'I had to call the doctor out again last night, because she had another episode of arrhythmia.' She sent him a troubled glance. 'I think it's the fact that her condition isn't consistent that's causing a dilemma for the consultant. He's reluctant to start her on anticoagulation therapy until the results of the tests come back, and we're still waiting on those.'

'How is she this morning?'

'A little better. Margaret is with her, otherwise I would have had to take time off. It's very difficult to know what to do for the best. I know something is badly wrong, but I feel as though my hands are tied while we're waiting for the medical reports.'

He came and put an arm around her, a warm, supportive gesture that took away some of the stress and made her feel for just a moment that maybe she wasn't entirely alone.

'Would you like me to have a word with the cardiology consultant? I know our cardiology specialist is looking after Jane, but sometimes he liaises with a doctor from the hospital in the next county. Mr Morrison is due to visit here one day next week to give a lecture, and I could put in a word and ask if he would talk to our man and see if he could get a look at Jane's file. He owes me a favour or two.'

'You don't think Dr Havers would object to that? I don't want to tread on anyone's toes.'

'No, I don't think there would be a problem.

Both men get on very well together, and neither of them will be put out if I ask them to look at Jane's case specifically, once they know that she's a friend of mine.'

Kayleigh nodded. 'Thank you...I would appreciate that. I just have this horrible feeling that we're not seeing the full picture, and I love my aunt to bits. I don't want anything to happen to her.'

'I'll see to it, then.' He gave her a squeeze and drew her a little closer to him. It was good, having him hold her this way, and for a reckless moment she found herself wondering how it would be if he was to be there for her all the time.

A rush of heat ran through her body. Clearly, she wasn't thinking straight. Of course he wasn't going to be around to pick up the pieces every time she fell apart—hadn't she learnt that she needed to look after herself? There was no reassurance to be had in relying on anyone else. Besides, he was only comforting her as he would have soothed any colleague in distress.

Lewis could be caring and considerate, but he was also her boss, and he wasn't the kind of man who would want to get involved in any deep and meaningful way. He was being compassionate towards her right now, but he could just as easily become distant, withdrawing into himself and giving the impression that he was as inaccessible as ever. There was a part of him that she could never reach.

She eased herself away from him, and he gave her a questioning look. 'Are you sure you're going to be all right?'

She nodded. 'I should go and see to my patients.'

'OK. I'll be around the corner in the next bay if you need me for any reason, though we seem to be having a relatively quiet day up to now.'

Kayleigh left him and went to examine a young man who had an injured shoulder. 'Are you able to move the arm at all?' she asked. She glanced at him. Something about him seemed familiar but she couldn't quite think how it was that she knew him.

He gritted his teeth. 'Not unless you want to hear a grown man scream. That might be offputting for some of the children around here.'

Kayleigh winced. 'You're probably right

about that. I'll prescribe some painkilling medication for you, and then when you're feeling a little more comfortable, we'll send you down to X-Ray so that we can see what's going on with the shoulder. It looks as though you've dislocated it, but we need to make sure there's no fracture or other kind of damage.'

'OK.' He looked at her. 'And then you can fix it for me?'

She nodded. 'With the help of a colleague, yes. I expect Dr McAllister will give me a hand as soon as we're ready.' She studied the notes. 'How did you do this exactly? It says here that it was a sporting accident.'

'That's right. I was waterskiing, but I didn't follow through properly and the boat in front that was pulling me went one way and I went the other, giving my arm a wrench in the process.' He grimaced. 'I thought water sports were supposed to be fun, but I guess I have to adjust my technique.'

Her mouth made a wry shape. 'I think that would be wise.'

Sharon came to assist her and now she handed the nurse the chart. 'I've written Mr Channing up for a painkiller, but we may have to add a sedative and an intravenous analgesic when he comes back from X-Ray.'

Sharon nodded and started to make arrangements for a porter to take the patient to Radiology.

When she had done that, she called Kayleigh over to the desk and said, 'While we're not so busy, I wanted to ask you about the fundraising we're doing for the children's ward. I've organised a guessing game, where we ask people to match the doctor with the parents, and there are small prizes for getting it right. I have all your details, about your father's software business, and your mother's work as a designer, but I'm struggling to find out anything about Lewis's background.'

She coughed and stopped to blow her nose on a paper tissue. 'He's always in the middle of something whenever I ask him—even this morning, he said, "Not now, Sharon…" But time's running on, and I have to get this sorted.' She grimaced. 'I heard a rumour that his family owned this massive corporation, but I don't know what they make or do. Do you have any idea?'

Kayleigh frowned. 'I think they have something to do with electronic systems—circuit boards for computers and sensor equipment, or something.'

'They don't use the family name, do they?'

Kayleigh shook her head. 'No, it's something like CC Technologies...I'm not exactly sure.'

'Say that again.' Sharon put her head to one side, listening for every word. 'I'm having some problems with my hearing today. My ears are blocked and my sinuses are giving me a headache.'

Kayleigh carefully repeated what she had said, but when Sharon started to write it down on her notepad, she had a tremor of doubt and said hastily, 'You know...I'm not sure that Lewis will want you to include any mention of his parents in this charity event. He gets a bit prickly whenever anything comes up about them. I wouldn't do anything without asking him first.'

Sharon gave a soft laugh. 'It's just a charity thing—no one's going to be upset by any of this. Besides, he said he would do whatever was needed...he agreed to take part.'

'Even so...'

The admissions clerk came over to them and handed Sharon a sheaf of papers. 'Will you sort through these and let me know which ones need to be passed on to the fracture clinic? They've just landed on my desk, but I don't know what to do with them, and Orthopaedics are shouting, saying they want them now.'

'Oh, drat. Yes, I'll see to it.' Sharon dropped her notepad into a wire tray and took the papers, running her free hand in a harassed fashion over her forehead. 'Everything in this place is last minute, and has to be done right now. Why am I doing this job?' She went away, shaking her head, just as Lewis came out of the treatment bay and into the main area of the unit.

Lewis walked over to the desk and started to rummage through the assortment of trays. 'Where are the lab-test results for my rheumatology patient?'

Kayleigh looked at him blankly, before she realised that Sharon's notebook was resting on top of them. She made to pick it up, but Lewis reached it first and studied it, his eyes darkening, a deep frown line appearing at the bridge of his nose.

'What's this?' He directed a penetrating stare towards Kayleigh.

'Um…I think it's something to do with the charity event—you know, they're trying to get funds for the new children's wing.'

'But this has my name on it.'

'Does it?' She tried to look unconcerned. 'Well, it's probably just a gathering of ideas for various activities that they're planning.'

He jabbed a finger on the page where Sharon had made her last few notes. 'This lists my father's company, and it says what they're about.' His jaw clenched. 'This is Sharon's writing, isn't it?'

'Is it?' It wasn't a lie. After all, she was just asking a question. She looked at him watchfully, passing the tip of her tongue over lips that were suddenly dry.

'There's only one place she could have got this information.' His gaze lanced into her. 'You must have given it to her. I haven't told anyone else about the company.'

'Haven't you?' Her eyes widened. It didn't look as though there was any way out of this, and she could see that he was getting angrier by the minute.

His voice became deadly soft, his eyes carrying a glitter that echoed his mood. 'I don't like having my private life laid open this way, just for some irritating quiz or entertainment. Neither do I appreciate you bandying this about to all and sundry.' He laid emphasis on each of his words. 'This is none of anyone's business. Do you understand that? Am I making myself clear?'

She nodded. She daren't open her mouth to speak because she was sure her voice would have deserted her in the face of his cold wrath, but just then she heard the unit's doors swish open and the porter was bringing her patient back from X-Ray.

She turned and made a feeble gesture towards the oncoming wheelchair.

His eyes narrowed. 'Go and see to him. But just so you know, I haven't finished with you,' he said darkly. 'I'll talk to you about this later.'

She winced, and then went to take over from the porter, wheeling the young man into the nearest available treatment cubicle. As she walked away, she was conscious of Lewis's stare piercing her back.

She tried to forget about him for the moment

and began to study the X-rays, putting them up on the light box. 'There isn't any fracture, Ben,' she said, 'so it's just a question of putting the shoulder back into position.' She hesitated. 'Just bear with me for a minute or two while I go and ask my colleague to help me with that.' Perhaps Lewis would be otherwise engaged by now, and Rob might be on hand to help out.

He wasn't. She explained the situation to Lewis and he walked to the treatment cubicle without saying a word to her. Perhaps he was still doing battle with his demons, and Kayleigh decided that the best thing she could do was to concentrate all her attention on her patient.

'As promised, I'm going to give you an injection of a strong painkiller first of all,' she told Ben. 'Are you ready for us to make a start?'

'As ready as I'll ever be,' Ben said. 'I'll be glad when this is over.'

Kayleigh gave him the injection, and while they waited for it to take effect, Lewis was carefully examining the shoulder. 'It's understandable that you're a feeling a little apprehensive,' he said, 'but it shouldn't be a difficult manoeuvre, and it will be over in a short time.'

'You know,' Kayleigh said, looking carefully at the young man, 'I'm sure I recognise you from somewhere. Have we met before this?'

'I think we have,' he agreed. 'Your face looks familiar to me, too.' He studied her for a second or two. 'My parents live in one of the stone cottages by the harbour. I lived there, too, until I went away to college in Cornwall. I've been staying in students' accommodation there for the last couple of years, but, of course, I come back and stay with my parents during vacations.'

'I expect we've seen each other around from time to time, then,' Kayleigh murmured. 'That would explain it. We must have grown up in the same area.'

Lewis signalled to Kayleigh that he was ready to start the procedure, and then he glanced at Ben and asked, 'Where do you do your water-skiing? I know of one major centre, but it's down by the popular surfers' beach some forty or so miles from here.'

There was a satisfying click as the shoulder popped back into position, and Ben gave a soft yelp, his eyes widening.

'Are you all right?' Lewis asked, studying Ben's reactions.

Ben sucked in a deep breath and then let it out again. 'I'm fine. The pain has gone—well, not gone, exactly, but it feels much better.' He looked pleased about that.

'That's good. That's what we like to hear,' Lewis said with a faint smile. 'We need to immobilise the shoulder now and put the arm in a sling, but before we let you go we'll do another X-ray, just to make sure that all is well. I need to do a neurological check, too. We'll give you some painkillers to take home with you, and you'll need to come back to see us in Outpatients for a check up.'

'Thanks.' Ben seemed to be getting himself back together after his ordeal. He said, as an afterthought, 'You were asking me about the waterskiing…and you're right, there is a centre near the surfers' beach. I tend to use it during term time, because my college isn't far from there, but I did this injury nearer to home.' He looked at Lewis. 'Are you keen on water sports?'

Lewis nodded. 'I am, but I don't always find

the time to indulge.' He frowned, and then asked, 'Since you and Dr Byford appear to know each other…I guess that means you must also know her younger sister?'

'That's right.' Ben glanced at Kayleigh. 'You and your sister look very much like one another, don't you? I think that's why I was a bit uncertain when I first saw you—I remembered seeing someone who looked a lot like you when I was back at college, but I expect it was your sister that I came across, and not you.'

Kayleigh's heart quickened. 'Was this recently that you saw her?'

'It was a few weeks ago. We had an open day at the college, and I think she must have come along to enquire about one of the courses. We didn't speak or anything, but I remember thinking that I knew her from somewhere. I think I've come across her once or twice since then, around the town.'

'So you wouldn't have any idea where she's living at the moment?' Kayleigh asked.

'I'm afraid not.' He glanced at her. 'It sounds as though you're trying to get in touch with her—have you lost her address or something?'

'Yes, that's right.' Kayleigh was still doing battle with her pulse rate. Her heart was thudding so much that it was almost painful. She said, 'At least now I know that she's probably living not too far away from here. I've been trying to find out where she is, but it's a start to know that you've seen her.' She flashed him a smile. 'I'm so glad that we saw you here today.'

'I'm quite pleased that I ran into you, too.' Ben glanced at his shoulder and his mouth made a rueful shape. 'Otherwise I might still be stranded with a useless arm.'

Lewis had already started the neurological examination, but when he had finished he handed Ben over to a nurse, with instructions to fix him up with a sling.

Kayleigh was writing up the chart, but she glanced up at Lewis and opened her mouth to speak. Lewis simply turned and walked away.

She guessed he was still angry with her, and for the rest of the day she did her best to keep out of his way.

Back at home, Aunt Jane was thrilled to hear about the patient who had seen her sister. 'It would be so good to have Heather back after all this time,' she said.

She paused to get her breath, and Kayleigh could see that heart was going into another bout of arrhythmia. 'I just feel so bad that she wasn't here when your mother passed away,' Aunt Jane went on. 'Is there anything I can do to help you to find her?'

'No, I'll do everything that needs to be done,' Kayleigh said. 'I'll drive down there and make some more enqui-ries.' She laid a gentle hand on her aunt's shoulder. 'You need to rest as much as possible and concentrate on getting yourself well again. I'll go and get your tablets for you. They should help.'

When she went into A and E the next morning, Lewis wasn't anywhere to be seen. 'I think he's gone over to the intensive care unit,' Sharon said. 'He wanted to check up on the little girl that came in the other day—you know, the girl in the cliff fall. She had a bad head injury, and I think he's been worrying about her ever since.' She frowned. 'He seemed to be in an odd sort of mood.'

'Did he?' Kayleigh's spirits plummeted, but

she thought it best not to make any comment on that score. 'I know he was concerned about the child. She wasn't doing too well, the last I heard. Lewis did everything he could, but she had been lying on that ledge for some time while the parents waited for the coastguard and the ambulance.'

She worked her way through her list of patients, but Lewis must have been busy with emergencies himself, because she didn't see anything of him for the entire morning.

Later, as she was glancing through some lab test results, the desk clerk called her to phone.

'Someone called Jacob is on the line,' she said.

'Thanks.' Kayleigh leaned back against the desk. 'Jacob,' she murmured, 'I'm glad you called. I've been trying to get in touch with you. I think we might have a clue to help us to find Heather. Someone has seen her.'

'That's why I'm calling. I got your messages, and I guessed that was what you wanted to tell me. I thought perhaps we could get together over lunch and have a chat about it, since I'm in the area. I don't know if you're free to do that today. There's a work experience group meeting by the river, and I've managed to slip away for an hour while a colleague takes over.' He hesitated. 'It would be good if you could tell me all about your news face to face. Maybe we could meet up at the Riverside Hotel. It's only across the way from the hospital, so I was hoping you might manage it. I'm over there right now.'

Kayleigh checked her watch. 'I should be going off duty in just a few minutes,' she said. 'I'll come and see you.'

She cut the call a second or two later, and went back to her test results, almost running into Lewis, who appeared out of nowhere and was glancing through some charts.

'I thought you were still with your stroke patient,' she said. 'Do you have time to look at some lab results with me? I'm going to lunch with Jacob, but I have a minute or two to spare to go through them if you can manage it.'

'I can't...not unless it's an emergency,' he said. 'I have to go and speak to the neurologist.'

His manner was strained, and she wasn't sure whether that was because of problems at work or because he was still annoyed with her, but she said, 'There's no rush. My patient still has to go for a scan. I'll see you later, when I get back from lunch.'

She hurried away. Jacob was waiting for her in the restaurant, and he had already secured a table by the window. They ordered an Italian dish, sun-dried tomatoes with eggs and cheese and a helping of pasta in a creamy sauce, and while they ate, she told him about Heather.

'It looks as though she might have been living near the bay for a few weeks at least. I'm sure we made enquiries over there when she first went missing, but nothing came of it back then.'

Jacob was thoughtful. 'It sounds as though she's planning on settling there—at least, it seems that way if she's enquiring about courses at the college.'

Kayleigh glanced at him. 'I was thinking of driving over there at the weekend. Do you want to come with me?'

He was hesitant at first, but then he shook his head. 'I don't think so. There's always the possibility that you might strike lucky and run into her, but it might not be such a good idea for me to meet up with her without warning. I don't know how she would react, and I still have trouble with the fact that she left so suddenly.' His mouth took on an awkward shape. 'I know I'm not always the easiest person to get along with, but she could have told me what was on her mind. There were things that we argued about, but I had hoped we might find a solution. Leaving the way she did, I didn't get a chance to talk things through with her.'

'I think we all have questions that we want answered,' Kayleigh said softly. 'You're probably right, and we should take this one step at a time.'

They didn't talk about Heather for the rest of the meal, and some time later, when Kayleigh looked at her watch and realised that it was time for her to go back to A and E, Jacob offered to walk with her. He was in a better mood by then, and she was teasing him because he wouldn't let her roll back his shirtsleeve and read some of the things that had been written on the cast on his arm.

'It's not your blushes I'm worried about,' he said. 'It's mine.'

He left her at the door to A and E, and gave her a light kiss on the cheek before he turned and made his way back to his own place of work. Kayleigh watched him go.

'Your patient is back from the CT scan,' Sharon told her, when she went to glance over her charts. 'Do you want to look at the films?'

'Yes, that would be a good idea...though I was hoping Lewis would come and look at them with me. I really wanted his advice on this patient's condition.'

Sharon made a face. 'Rather you than me. I don't seem to be his favourite person right now—though I suppose I might have that all wrong. It might be that he's still concerned about the little girl with the head injury. He came back from the intensive care unit looking a bit out of sorts.' She sniffed, then coughed and rubbed at her eyes. Glancing across the room, she saw that Lewis was heading their way.

'I'm going to make myself scarce,' she said, rubbing the back of her hand across her forehead.

Lewis came to take a file from the tray, flicking a sideways glance at Kayleigh. 'So you're back from your lunch-break, then. I wasn't sure how long you would be.' There was a flat edge to his voice, and his eyes were dark, as though his mind was elsewhere.

She narrowed her gaze. 'I don't usually take extra time.' She picked up the CT films and said, 'Would you take a look at these with me? They're for the patient I asked you about earlier. I'd appreciate it if you would look at the lab test results, too.'

He nodded, and walked with her over to the annexe, where she put the films up on the light box.

He studied them for a while, and then pointed out an area of calcification on the films. 'That's a kidney stone. What's the problem with the lab tests?'

'There are one or two discrepancies…I'd like your opinion.'

He tugged the films from the light box and handed them to her. 'You need to ask for a consultation with a renal surgeon. I'll take a look at the test results, but I can tell you now that this won't be resolved with medication alone. Your patient will have to go for surgery.'

She nodded. 'I'll arrange for him to see a specialist.'

She would have turned away then, but he stopped her, saying, 'How did your lunch with Jacob go?'

'It was all right. He seemed a bit down in himself to begin with, but I think I managed to cheer him up a bit.'

He nodded. 'I saw you come back to A and E with him, and he looked fine then. I'm surprised to hear you say that he wasn't in good form. I would have expected him to be glad that you have some news about your sister.'

Kayleigh wrinkled her nose. 'You'd think so, wouldn't you, but he looked to me as though he was a bit apprehensive about the whole thing. Of course, it may be that he's afraid we won't actually find her. Perhaps he doesn't want to get his hopes up and then be disappointed.'

'Or he may be wondering if she'll expect to kiss and make up. Perhaps he doesn't want to do that. He said he didn't think he was ready for commitment back then, before she went away, didn't he?'

'Did he?' Her brows met in a frown.

'That's what he told me when I spoke to him.'

She sent him an uncertain look. His jaw was

tense, and he seemed to be in a grim kind of mood, just as Sharon had said. 'I didn't know that you had spoken to him on your own.'

He nodded. 'He came in one day to find out how the boy from the burns unit was doing. I think you were down in the lab, chasing up some tests.'

'Oh, I see.' He obviously hadn't thought fit to mention it to her that Jacob had been around. 'I thought it was good of him to take the time to talk to Craig and persuade him that he should see his mother and make things up with her.'

'Yes, I've noticed that you tend to see the best in people...your stepfather excluded, of course.' There was a wry inflection in his tone that made her flick him a quick look.

'Are you saying that I'm wrong to be that way?'

'Not at all. I just think that in general you tend to see people through rose-tinted spectacles. You're putting great store in finding your sister, but I wonder if you've thought of the downside to all this?'

'What downside? I didn't think there was one.'

'No?' He grimaced. 'Just supposing you were

to find your sister...what will you do if she doesn't want to be reunited with her family? After all, she left of her own accord, and she might be perfectly happy to be left alone to get on with her life. She may not want you to interfere.'

Kayleigh glared at him. 'I'm not interfering. How can you say something like that?'

'Aren't you? Who are you to say that she's not content as she is? What makes you so sure that you know best?'

Her mouth tightened. 'I know that family is important...that we need people around us to make us complete and to help out when things get tough. I'm sorry for you if you don't feel that way, but I look at things differently from you.' She pulled in a deep breath. 'I'm going to find my sister whether you agree with me or not.'

She turned away from him and tried to quell the rising tide of despair that was growing inside her. He would never understand. For all that he had offered to help originally, he didn't have an ounce of family feeling. He was like an alien, an interloper among humanity, a man without a soul.

CHAPTER EIGHT

'I THINK Lewis is wrong,' Aunt Jane said, spreading marmalade on her toast and glancing across the breakfast table at Kayleigh. 'If there's any chance at all that we might be able to find Heather, we should follow it through.' She paused and swallowed, staying silent for a moment as though she was waiting for the toast to disappear. 'She's our flesh and blood and we need to know that she's safe and well. I can't see either of us resting until we've been reassured of that.'

'That's what I thought.' Kayleigh murmured. She was still cross with Lewis for suggesting that she might be jumping in with both feet where she wasn't wanted, and it was helpful to know that Aunt Jane thought she was doing the right thing. At the very least, she planned on driving over to Cornwall on her next day off, so that she could make a few more enqui-ries about where her sister might be staying.

She couldn't imagine what made Lewis so determined to hold back from people. It was such a paradox, when he worked with people every day, and had to care for them in all sorts of circumstances, and yet in some ways he could be downright cynical in his outlook.

'There's more to our man next door than meets the eye,' Aunt Jane said. 'He's as good as gold with me, but I know he can be a bit austere at times, as though he wants to be left alone. He gets that distant look in his eyes and I know to leave him to himself.'

Kayleigh finished off her own piece of toast and wiped her hands on a serviette. 'I shall certainly be leaving him alone. I thought I was getting to know him and understand what goes on in his head, but I'm finished with trying to figure men out. Either they stifle you with constant attention, and then they think that gives them the right to take over and run things, or they play it cool and think a woman will fall at their feet. Well, that's not for me, not any more. I was beginning to think that Lewis was different, but he isn't.' Her mouth made a straight line. 'I'll stick with being independent and doing things my way. I'm better off on my own.'

Aunt Jane made a face. 'You've had a few bad experiences, love. You shouldn't let that colour your judgment.' She fell silent, swallowing again, and Kayleigh sent her a swift glance.

'Are you feeling all right?'

Aunt Jane nodded. 'I'm just feeling a little nauseous…it'll pass. I shouldn't have had that last piece of toast.'

'But you look as though you're in pain. Tell me where it hurts…'

'I'll be fine in a minute or two. It was just a twinge.'

'Are you sure? You're very pale. Do you want me to stay with you today, instead of going in to work?'

'I'm sure. There's nothing wrong with me but a spot of indigestion.'

Kayleigh frowned. She wasn't entirely convinced that her aunt was telling her the truth, but she said softly, 'Will you promise me that you'll call me at work if you feel unwell in any way? I shall worry if I think you're in pain or having problems of any kind. I'll come back home straight away if you need me...you know that, don't you?'

'I do, love, but I'm all right, really. Anyway, you know Margaret comes and keeps an eye on me every day. She doesn't leave me on my own for very long without checking that I'm OK. You don't have to worry about me at all.'

'I hope that's true.' Kayleigh was a little concerned all the same. Perhaps she would give her aunt a ring later on to make sure that all was well.

At work, an hour or so later, she soon became resigned to the fact that things were not running smoothly. An influx of patients from a road accident stretched their resources, and Sharon had the look of someone who needed to be in several places at once. She was hurrying about the place with a distracted air and when Lewis stopped to talk to her for a moment or two her expression changed to one of anxiety. That was odd, Kayleigh thought.

She caught up with the nurse as she was about to head along the corridor towards the store-room when the worst of the rush was over. 'Are you bearing up?' she asked. 'It's been hectic this morning, hasn't it?'

Sharon stood still, sending Kayleigh an oblique glance. She looked fraught, her expression taking on a haunted tinge. 'It's chaotic, and just to make things more difficult, there's a little boy wandering about the place. He keeps coming in from the waiting room while his mother isn't looking.' She coughed and then winced. 'I suppose we can't be too hard on her because she's worried about her husband. I must say, he didn't look well at all.'

'At least you've taken the trouble to talk to her.'

Sharon nodded. 'Now we're running low on dressings. I'm just going to see if there's been a new delivery in the last day or so. I might be able to stock up the shelves in the store cupboard now that we have five minutes to breathe.'

Perhaps she had spoken too soon, because just then a commotion started up in the waiting room, and within minutes Lewis was calling for a crash team. A man was lying on the floor, not breathing, in cardiac arrest. He was young, in his early thirties, Kayleigh judged, and it seemed strange that a fit-looking man should succumb to something as serious as this. A little boy, about four years old, wandered into A and E, his eyes wide, taking everything in. He was sucking on a sweet, his cheeks pulled in and his mouth puckered up.

Kayleigh hurried towards the man who had collapsed, along with Rob, the junior doctor, ready to start chest compressions and give him oxygen. Sharon came with them, but Lewis said sharply, 'No, not you, Sharon. Take that child away from here and see if you can find his mother or a relative.'

Lewis was already working with the patient, putting in an airway, calling for another nurse to charge the defibrillator. With the paddles in place, he gave the first shock to try to convert the heart to normal rhythm.

He glanced at the monitor. 'Again,' he said.

'Charging.'

'Clear.' Lewis gave another shock to the patient's heart. He went on trying to save the man, giving him adrenaline through an intravenous line, and Kayleigh was beginning to be fearful that their efforts were going to come to nothing.

Then, at last, he said, 'That's good, we have a pulse. Let's get him into a side room, and start finding out what caused this.' He called to the registrar to take over.

As they wheeled the young man away, Lewis glanced across the room and saw that Sharon was hovering in the doorway.

He frowned. 'Why are you still here, Sharon? I told you earlier, I don't want to see you in A and E.' Lewis used a curt tone, and the nurse blinked, giving him a dismayed stare.

'You said I should take the boy to his mother, but she's not up to looking after him. She's worried about her husband.' She pointed to the man they had just brought back from the brink of death. Then she turned away, holding a tissue to her face, and Kayleigh thought she looked as though she was trying to hold back tears.

Then Rob called urgently for assistance, and Lewis hurried over to him to see what was wrong. The four-year-old child who had been wandering about was making strange noises and spluttering, bending forward in a jerking

sort of motion. Kayleigh pulled in a quick
breath, her abdomen tightening.

'The boy's choking,' Rob said. 'I've tried everything I can think of—back blows and chest thrusts.
Whatever's blocking his airway isn't shifting.'

It looked as though the boy was in desperate
trouble. His mother stood by, looking on in
anguish while Lewis checked his mouth to see
if he could locate the obstruction.

'He was rummaging about in my bag,' the
mother said, her voice dissolving tearfully. 'I
didn't notice until it was too late.'

Lewis and Rob were still struggling to
dislodge whatever was causing the problem.

'Nothing's working,' Rob said in a low voice,
his face deathly pale. 'What do we do next? Is
there any way we can open up the airway?'

'We might have to try a needle cricothyroi-
dotomy.' Lewis was still attempting to dislodge
whatever it was that was causing the blockage,
and he, too, was grim-faced. Kayleigh watched
from a distance as the child began to slip into unconsciousness. The day was going from bad to
worse.

Lewis reached for a laryngoscope and looked

down the child's throat once again, pressing the boy's tongue out of the line of vision and allowing a small light to illuminate the airway. Rob handed him some forceps and a moment later Lewis gave a soft sound of relief. Triumphantly he held the forceps aloft, their metal prongs gripping on to a boiled sweet.

'Let's get him on oxygen right away,' he said. 'He should start to recover soon.'

Kayleigh's shoulders slumped as she let the tension seep out of her and then, collecting her thoughts, she began to look around for Sharon. The nurse was hurrying away in the direction of the staff locker rooms, and Kayleigh went after her, worrying in case she was upset.

She found Sharon collecting her things together and stuffing them into a holdall.

'Are you all right?' She looked at the young woman, who glanced up from the holdall and tucked a strand of hair behind her ear. Her eyes looked puffy and reddened, and her face was flushed.

Sharon nodded. 'I'm going home. I know I should have gone earlier, but there was so much to do, and now Lewis is annoyed with me.' She sniffed. 'I still haven't finished checking the drugs cupboard, and the dressings that we ordered have got lost somewhere. I can't just leave everything…we're short-staffed as it is.'

Kayleigh shook her head. 'I'm sure Lewis will find someone else to take over. He's told you to go, so now that's his responsibility.' She frowned. 'What happened? Why is he annoyed with you? I thought he'd got over the business of the charity event.' She wasn't exactly clear on that, but there was no point in upsetting Sharon any further.

'I suppose so. I don't know. But I collected the wrong films from X-Ray, and then I sent his patient to Rheumatology instead of Neurology, and he had words with me about it. He wasn't very pleased.' She started to cough. 'And now he must think I left the little boy to wander about and get into mischief.'

'Oh, dear.' Kayleigh frowned. 'I doubt he thinks that, and you shouldn't let it distress you. We all make mistakes from time to time, don't we? Besides, you don't look well, and you'll probably find that you'll be better off at home. You should try to get some rest.'

Sharon nodded. 'My head's a bit muzzy, that's all. I'll be fine.' She didn't look as though that was true, but she shut the door of her locker and turned the key. 'Will you tell him about the drugs cupboard and the dressings? I tried to tell him myself, but he told me to go.'

'I'll sort it.' Kayleigh watched Sharon go out of the room and then she went off in search of Lewis, her grey eyes sparking. He had no right to treat people that way.

He was coming out of one of the treatment bays as she returned to A and E, and he turned towards the staff rest room, flicking through a folder of what looked like management bumph as he went.

She followed him into the room and shut the door behind them. The room was empty, but there was a pot of coffee simmering on a hotplate in the alcove and Lewis went over there to help himself to a cup.

He started to frown. 'There's no milk,' he said. 'Who keeps taking all the milk?'

'I've no idea,' she said in a taut voice. 'You'll just have to take your coffee black, won't you? It will probably suit your mood.' She still hadn't forgiven him for daring to suggest that she should leave her sister to get by on her own.

His head went back. 'Have I done something to upset you?'

Her eyes widened. 'Do you want a list? We could start with yesterday, if you like, and go into how you slated me for daring to say that your father worked in electronic circuitry.' She glared at him. 'As though that's the crime of the century.'

His mouth compressed, and he sent her a warning look. 'Let's not go there.'

'Oh, that bothers you, does it? I'd better not offend your sensibilities, had I?' She straightened her back, warming to her theme. 'Not that it matters if you, for your part, upset the nursing staff, of course. That's a different matter entirely, isn't it?'

She glowered at him, and then realised that perhaps there were mitigating circumstances. She said more calmly, 'Though I suppose you could be forgiven for being such an insensitive person if it came about because you were distracted, or worried about something...the little girl in Intensive Care, perhaps? I heard that she was still under sedation.'

'There's no real news yet.' His brows drew together. 'What gives you the idea that I'm in any way insensitive?'

She pretended to think about that. 'Well, let me see...your manner over the last couple of days has been less than perfect and verging on the chilly side, I'd say, and Sharon looks shattered, as though you've just torn a strip off her. She's very upset. She's worried about the drugs cupboard not being checked and the fact that we're understaffed, and she also has the charity event to organise.'

He looked at her steadily. 'Have you finished?'

'No, I haven't.' She gritted her teeth. 'She's not feeling too good and she feels that you're annoyed with her. I'm sure she doesn't deserve any censure at all. She's a good nurse, and she's usually very dependable.'

'Since when did you become an expert on staff relations?' He pressed his lips together. 'We didn't have words. I asked her why she had brought me the wrong X-ray films, but she didn't appear to know what I was talking about.' His jaw tightened. 'I'm supposed to be in charge here and that means I have to be sure that everything is running smoothly. If it isn't, or if there's a major glitch in the system, I'm the one who is responsible for sorting it out. Do you have a problem with that? Or perhaps you think you would make a better job of dealing with the staff and the patients?'

She took a step backwards and held up her hands as though to ward him off. 'Let's hold on, there, shall we? If we're talking about job suitability, does it ever occur to you that you might be the one to have chosen the wrong career?'

He blinked, his head going back, and then stared at her, his blue eyes glittering. 'I beg your pardon?' The words came out as though they were being crunched between his teeth.

She made a negligent shrug. 'Well, where is all this attitude coming from? Only the other day you were telling me that you passed over the chance to work in the family business in order to go into medicine, and yet here you are, acting as though you hate the job, as though it's a huge burden all of a sudden. What am I supposed to think?'

His gaze narrowed on her. 'Oh, that's very

clever, isn't it? Are you doing your best to wind me up?'

She returned his stare. 'Would I do that? Perhaps you'd prefer it if I kept my thoughts to myself.'

His mouth made an odd twist. 'I doubt that would be possible.'

She raised a brow. 'Really?' She used a sarcastic tone. 'I'm crushed...I think.'

He said tersely, 'So you should be. Perhaps you'd do better to think things through a little before you make comments like that. Where Sharon is concerned, I told her to go home because she was unwell. She has a head cold, which means she can't hear properly, and she's passing on her germs to all and sundry. I'd much rather she stayed away until she's feeling better.'

'Oh.' Kayleigh felt suddenly deflated. 'I didn't realise that.'

'So I gathered.' He gave her a hard stare. 'As for me going into medicine...I've never for one moment regretted becoming a doctor. I had good reason for making that career choice.'

She sent him a hesitant glance. 'I remember you saying something about that...wasn't it a child at school who was taken ill? What happened? It must have had a dramatic effect on you.'

He looked at her steadily. 'It did. He was my best friend, John.'

'The same John whose house you're living in?'

'That's right. He's the one.'

She realised that must have been a firm friendship to have lasted so long. 'So, what happened?'

He made a face. 'He collapsed in the classroom and I was scared to death that he wouldn't pull through. He was lying on the floor, going blue around the lips from lack of oxygen.'

'That must have been scary.'

'Yes, it was. The teacher wanted to clear the room of children, but he couldn't do that and resuscitate John and call the ambulance all at the same time. I offered to help, so he showed me how to assist with the resuscitation attempts while one of the other boys went to get some more staff members. Between us, we managed to keep him alive until the paramedics arrived.'

Kayleigh was quiet, imagining how traumatic that experience must have been for a young boy. 'It sounds as though it was a life-changing experience.'

'It was for me. I knew then that nothing was ever going to be more important to me than trying to save lives. John was my friend, but he almost died that day.'

'So that's why you went on to argue with your father about working for the family company? You must have had a very strong conviction about what you needed to do.'

His mouth made a wry twist. 'I'd say that was true enough. I certainly didn't believe that I would be content to spend my life shifting electronic components from one end of the globe to another.'

Kayleigh was oddly subdued. 'It seems strange that your parents couldn't see how motivated you were. They must have listened to your side of the story and made some attempt to understand your point of view, surely…your mother, especially? Wouldn't she have put in a word for you?'

She knew that she shouldn't have said it as soon as the words came out of her mouth. She was treading on dangerous ground after he had said the other day that he didn't want to talk about his mother, but there had to be a limit to how much he could keep buried inside him. 'After all,' she said haltingly, 'it's possible that men can sometimes be blinkered where ambition is concerned, but their wives can often turn them around and show them a different way.'

'Maybe, but that didn't apply in my case. My parents were too busy putting their own business plans into operation, and they certainly didn't pay any attention to what I had to say. I had the strong feeling that they didn't want the bother of having me around. Perhaps they hadn't planned on having a child, and I was simply in the way.'

Kayleigh was shocked. 'That's a harsh judgment, don't you think? They were your parents, for better or worse, and surely they must have wanted the best for you. Isn't that why your father wanted you to be part of the family firm? That would all have been part of the caring, his way of showing you that you were important to him.'

His expression was cynical. 'You'd think so, wouldn't you? If that was the case, why did they send me away to boarding school? I didn't want to go. I was seven years old when I first went away, and it wasn't just for a five-day week, it was for a whole term at a time.'

Kayleigh's mouth had dropped open in disbelief at what he was telling her, but now she worked it back into a semblance of normality.

She stared at him. 'There must have been some happy times. Weren't there?' Her voice trailed away. 'What about the summer holidays, when school was closed?'

He shrugged. 'They were often abroad and couldn't get back...or maybe they didn't trouble themselves to get back. They blamed pressure of business, deals that were make or break or that needed their undivided attention, and so on. It was all for my good, for my future, they said.' He made a face. 'I wanted to believe them, but I didn't really understand why they couldn't be with me. In the earlier years I went to stay with my grandparents, but they were old and frail, and after they passed away I would spend a good part of the summer months with John's parents. They felt that I had a part in saving his life, and I suppose that's why they took me in.'

Her mouth was open again, but now she

clamped it shut. What he had told her had an overwhelming effect on her. Surely it was no wonder that he was sometimes distant? When he had never known the unconditional, absolute love of his mother and father, the people who should have nurtured him throughout his growing years. More than anything, she wanted to reach out to him to hold him and show him that she cared.

'I can't imagine how that must have been for you,' she said, her voice husky with emotion. 'How could you bear being sent away like that? You were so young.' She desperately wanted to wrap her arms around him and comfort the inner child, and try to take away some of the hurt, but when she lifted her hand to touch his arm, he turned away and shook her off.

'I've told you before...don't try to smother me with your womanly sympathy. It doesn't work for me and I don't need it. If I have anything to thank my parents for, it's that I've learned that being independent is good. I'm my own person. I don't have to answer to anyone, and I like being on my own, making decisions that are for me alone.'

His mouth was taut. 'You said yourself, I'm not a receptive, soulful kind of man. Insensitive—wasn't that the word you used? Perhaps it's true. I am who I am, and you have to accept that.'

Kayleigh swallowed hard and bent her head, not looking at him. She was trying to fight off an surge of emotion that welled up in her throat and threatened to wash her eyes with tears.

How could she help him if he wouldn't admit to needing anyone or anything? Perhaps he would never accept that his life could be different, that she might be the one to show him all the joy and love and laughter that he had missed.

Her hands were trembling, and she struggled to get a grip on herself. Love…? Was that what she really felt for him? What was she doing, even thinking about him that way, daring to think about love having any part in her life where he was concerned?

She knew that it would be disastrous to allow herself to fall for someone like Lewis. She had always hoped that one day she would find a man who would be everything to her, who would warm her heart and who would give her the children she always wanted, but Lewis couldn't be the man to do that.

She couldn't possibly let herself fall in love with someone who kept his emotions locked up inside himself, could she? The question echoed through her mind...wasn't it already too late for that?

CHAPTER NINE

KAYLEIGH was still smarting from Lewis's rejection of her when she went to examine her next patient, a young woman who was around seven months pregnant and who had been brought in after a fall. She was complaining of a bad headache and dizziness.

Kayleigh took the woman's blood pressure and thought about all that Lewis had told her of his early years. Even now, she couldn't see why he had been so harsh in his attitude towards her. Why was it so wrong that she would want to offer him comfort and understanding?

Everything that was in her made her feel that she could do something to take away his inner pain, but instead of accepting her efforts to assuage his torment he had reacted by turning away from her and brushing her off as though she was a pesky fly, a nuisance, or at the very least an irritant. Just thinking about it brought a lump to her throat. How could she have let her guard down that way and opened herself up to hurt?

'Your blood pressure is very high, Maria,' she told the young woman, 'and your ankles look as though they're swollen and puffy. Considering the fact that there was protein in your urine, and that you're quite far into your pregnancy, I think at this stage we should do a few more tests to help us to see what's going on.'

She started to write up a blood test form. Perhaps it was true that he didn't need anyone. She knew what it was to be hurt, but she was a woman, with a woman's instincts and emotions, and maybe she had been wrong in thinking that it must be the same for him. He said that he had learned to be independent and that he liked being on his own, and it could be that he had succeeded where she had failed.

'Tests? What kind of tests?' Maria looked worried.

Kayleigh brought her attention back to her patient. 'None that you need to worry about. We'll do a blood test and an ECG trace first of all, and of course we need to monitor the baby to make sure it's doing all right. At any rate, we'll need to admit you for a day or two so that we can keep an eye on you.'

Maria's face fell. 'I don't like being in hospital, away from my family.' She moved restlessly on the bed.

'I know it's not the best place to be, Maria, but you need to do this for your own sake, and for your baby.'

Maria subsided, leaning back against her pillows. 'I suppose you're right.'

Kayleigh went to call for the obstetrician to come down and take a look at her patient, but the doctor was in Theatre, busy with an emergency Caesarean section.

Reluctantly, she went in search of Lewis. He was with the registrar, attending to the cardiac-arrest patient, but he acknowledged her with a faint nod, and Kayleigh waited for him to finish what he was doing. Her mood was simmering, shifting between chagrin at having shown him that she cared and anxiety because her defences had crumbled in such an abysmal fashion. For a long time she had tried to build a wall around herself, so that no one could get through to her and open up old wounds.

She knew better than to trust in men. When had they ever given her cause to feel that she was safe, that she could open her heart up to them and know that she would come to no harm?

'Is there a problem?' he asked.

She nodded, jerked out of her reverie by the deep timbre of his voice. 'I've a patient who is pregnant and showing signs of pre-eclampsia, but the obstetrician is tied up with an emergency right now, and I need specialist help. I have the woman on oxygen, but she's hypertensive and agitated and I'm afraid that her condition might deteriorate.' She didn't look him in the eyes and her jaw was taut.

'I'll come and take a look at her,' he said.

She didn't want to have to talk to him, but she was concerned about the man who had collapsed earlier, and as they walked back to the treatment bay she said in a clipped voice, 'How's your patient doing?'

'He'll be all right. His heart had slowed right down, and this is not the first time it's happened, apparently. We'll fit him with a pacemaker. That should get him back on track.'

'I'm glad.' Her manner was subdued. 'They were a very young family.'

'Yes, they were.' He sent her a swift, assessing look. 'I can see how his wife would have been preoccupied. It must have been a worrying situation for her.'

She nodded, but didn't say anything, and perhaps her sombre mood had filtered through to him because he said, 'You seem to be a little out of sorts…is that because of something I've done?'

'Oh, you've developed an extra sense, have you?' Her tone was sharp. 'I had no idea you could be so perceptive.'

He winced. 'I think I may have been a bit short with you, earlier…'

She lifted a brow. 'May have been?'

The wince turned into a grimace. 'Well, all right, I was perhaps a touch edgy with you. There's been no let-up all day and we're short-staffed, which doesn't help my temperament.' He shot her a quick look. 'You have to learn to handle differences of opinion and brusque comments when you work in this kind of environment.'

She shot him a frowning glance. Was that meant to be some kind of apology? If that was the case, she'd certainly heard better ones.

There was no time to let him know what she thought, though, because by now they had reached Maria's treatment bay, just as the nurse was hurrying towards them to say that the patient was beginning to convulse.

Kayleigh rushed over to the bedside, but Lewis was already calling for diazepam. He gave it to the woman intravenously, and after a moment or two the fitting stopped.

'Her blood pressure is still too high,' he murmured, glancing at Kayleigh. 'I'm going to add hydralazine to her medication. It'll be a few minutes before it takes effect.' To the nurse, he said, 'Call the obstetrician again, and ask her to come down here as soon as possible. The patient will have to be monitored closely, and if her condition doesn't improve, she may need to have a C-section so that we can deliver the baby. We can't risk her going into eclampsia or we could lose both her and the infant.' He pressed his lips together. 'At least she's more than twenty-eight weeks into the pregnancy, so the baby will stand a fighting chance.'

The nurse went off to make the call, and Lewis told Kayleigh, 'If she starts to fit again, add phenytoin to the diazepam.' He checked the monitors. 'From the looks of her, though, she seems to be stable for the moment.'

He frowned. 'I should go back to my other patients, and then I have to rearrange the duty rosters. With Sharon going off duty and some of the junior doctors on leave, I think we may be short on cover for the weekend…is there any chance that you'll you be available to work then if need be?'

She shook her head. 'I was planning on driving down to Cornwall to see if I can trace my sister.'

His eyes narrowed a fraction. 'I suppose Jacob will be going with you. He must have thought it through by now and decided that he wants to be there.'

'No, I'm going on my own. He didn't think it would be a good idea for him to go looking for her. He seems to be having mixed feelings about Heather just now, and he's not sure how she would react to seeing him again.'

He gave her a searching look. 'That's going to be difficult for you, isn't it? It could be quite a daunting task, doing it all on your own.'

'Yes, you're probably right, but it's something I feel I have to do.'

He was quiet for a moment. 'I could go with you, if you like. Two heads will most likely be better than one, and you might find that you need some support.'

'Are you sure that you want to do that?' His offer had taken her by surprise, given his comments about interference, but her treacherous heart made a small leap all the same. Was this his way of making amends for what had happened earlier?

Despite all her reservations, she had to acknowledge that it would be good to have him go with her. For all that she had been prepared to do it on her own, she knew that she would feel so much better with him by her side. He was capable and confident in whatever he undertook, and with any luck some of that confidence would transmit itself to her.

Even so, she said doubtfully, 'What about

the weekend rota? Won't you have trouble working it out?'

'I'll bring staff in from the agencies if need be. Don't worry about it. I'll come and pick you up first thing on Saturday.'

Kayleigh couldn't help herself...she was pleased at the prospect. His offer was so unexpected, especially after the way things had gone wrong between them. One part of her was thrilled that he would be coming with her, and another was apprehensive about how it would all turn out. What if despite all their efforts they couldn't find Heather?

When Saturday dawned, Kayleigh made sure that the arrangements she had made with Margaret next door were in place for her to keep a close eye on Aunt Jane.

'You don't need to get someone in to watch over me,' Aunt Jane objected. 'I'll get along fine on my own.'

Kayleigh frowned. 'I expect you will, but you like being with Margaret, don't you? She said you were great friends.'

'Yes, that's true…we are, but I don't want to put her out in any way.'

Kayleigh smiled. 'I don't think she looks on it that way. She said she was looking forward to going out to sit with you in the park for an hour or so, if you're up to it, and then she thought you might both come back here and play Scrabble.'

Aunt Jane smiled. 'Ah, yes, well, we both enjoy that.'

'So, do you think you'll be all right while I'm away?' Kayleigh was concerned about her aunt's pale features, and she thought that she was looking more tired than usual.

Aunt Jane patted her hand. 'I'll be just fine, love. Don't you worry. You concentrate on finding our Heather. That will make me feel on top of the world, if you manage to get to know where she is. And tell that young man of yours to take it easy on the drive down there. I want you both to stay safe.'

Kayleigh made a wry smile. 'He isn't my young man.'

'Hah…then why is he round here so often? Tell me that.'

'Because he wants to make sure that you're

all right. He thinks the world of you. You know he does.'

Aunt Jane's mouth curved. 'He's a good man. One of the best.' She must have caught Kayleigh's quizzical expression, because she added in a light tone, 'He's all right, in spite of his being a bit detached sometimes.'

Margaret came to sit with Aunt Jane, and Kayleigh showed her into the sitting room. The two women were soon chatting away and while Kayleigh went to switch on the kettle for a cup of tea.

Lewis arrived just a few minutes later, and when Kayleigh opened the door to him he stood for a moment and simply stared at her, not moving a muscle.

'Is something wrong?' Kayleigh asked.

He shook his head. 'No, nothing at all…absolutely nothing at all.' He looked her over and murmured, 'I'm used to seeing you in jeans and tops most weekends, and you always look good, but today you're…stunning…beautiful, and fresh like a summer breeze.'

She gave a soft laugh. 'And there are times when you have a way with words.' She was pleased that he liked the way she looked, all the same. Her clothes matched her mood. Her cotton skirt was light and cool, and her close-fitting top was sleeveless, with thin straps to allow the sun to caress her bare shoulders. 'It's such a warm day, and I feel sort of light-headed and expectant. For the first time, I feel that I have a good chance of finding my sister.'

He returned her smile, and as she drank in his long, lean shape, it occurred to her that he was pretty dazzling himself. He was wearing olive coloured chinos and a pale-coloured shirt that followed the line of his muscular chest and emphasised the flatness of his stomach.

'Are you ready to go?' he asked.

She nodded, and they set off in good time, after Kayleigh had left last-minute instructions about medication and meals.

'I've made up a light lunch for both of you,' she told Margaret, 'but don't worry if Aunt Jane's not very hungry. She had another bout of palpitations yesterday, and just lately she's been a bit sick and a little unwell around mealtimes, so she might not want to eat very much.'

'I'll make sure that she's all right. Don't you

worry.' Margaret stood by the front door and waved them off.

Lewis manoeuvred the car on to the main road just a few minutes later. 'At least we can start making more specific enquiries about your sister now that we have something to go on,' he said. 'It should be easier to check the official registers and so on to see if she's staying locally.'

'I was thinking the same thing,' Kayleigh agreed. She was pleased about this whole turn of events, but now that it was beginning to look as though she might be able to find her sister, the niggling thought struck her that Lewis might be right in what he had said before. There was always the chance that Heather might not react so well to being found.

She pulled in a deep breath. That was one bridge that she would have to cross when she came to it.

When they arrived in the seaside town some time later, they made enquiries at the offices where the official records were kept, but there was no information to be had, and they drew a blank.

'Perhaps your sister didn't register,' the clerk said. 'She may not have been here all that long...or perhaps she didn't want to be found.' He gave her a sympathetic look.

Kayleigh was devastated. She had pinned all her hopes on this day, and it simply wasn't turning out as she had planned.

'That was just the first hurdle,' Lewis said, putting an arm around her as they walked out on to the street. 'We could go and check with the employment offices, just in case she has her name down on their list.'

'They'll be closed today, won't they?'

'That's true. We may have to find an internet café in order to do that. We may not be able to find her, but we can look at the type of work she might be after, and follow up by visiting any companies that are local at some point, just to see if she has been to see them.'

A couple of hours later, they still hadn't made any headway. They walked along the sea front and watched the water wash up on to the shore and break up against the cliffs, sending up small showers of white spray.

'I don't know what more we can do,' Kayleigh

said despondently. 'We've tried looking at accommodation that's been rented out in the last few months, and holiday cottages, and so on, and we've come up with nothing. Perhaps Ben was wrong in thinking that he'd seen her...or maybe she's using a different name.'

Lewis was thoughtful. 'Maybe, but there is one thing we haven't tried.'

She sent him an oblique glance. 'What's that?'

'Ben mentioned the college. He said that she'd been there to enquire about courses...which makes me wonder if they might have kept a record of her visit. It's possible that she signed up for a course, after all, in which case they would have contact details.'

Her eyes widened. 'You're right. Why didn't I think of that?'

He smiled. 'Because you're too close to the situation...because you've been doing similar searches to this over such a long time and now you're tired and emotional about the whole thing.'

They drove to the college and looked around for anyone who might be able to supply them with information. Being the weekend, the main offices were closed, and there was only one clerk who was available to deal with any enquiries.

'Some of the students are resident here,' she told them, 'so we keep one office open in case they have any problems or queries. I'm not sure how I might be able to help you.' She hesitated. 'You have to realise that any information that we have on students is confidential.'

'I'm not sure that my sister is a student here,' Kayleigh explained, 'but one of your students remembered her coming to the college to ask about enrolment.' She told the woman about her predicament. 'I'm desperate to find her. I haven't seen her in three years and it's as though she's disappeared completely. This is the first sighting we've had of her in all that time.'

'Hmm…I'm not sure what the protocol would be here. I'm not supposed to reveal contact details, you see, except in an emergency—though I imagine family members might be exempt.' It was clear that the clerk was torn about which way to act. She was thoughtful for a moment, and then she said, 'I'll have a look in the enrolment book, and see if her name's listed there. Just bear with me for a moment.'

She went away and searched in a filing cabinet. After a while, she came back, holding a book, which she opened out, and then she started to flick through the pages.

'Byford…that was the name you said, wasn't it?' She laid the book down on the table in front of them, its pages open to view. 'We usually make a note of people who've asked to be on our mailing list in this book. Then when a place becomes available on a course, we can let them know.'

She looked thoughtful for a moment. 'I think I'll just leave the book there for a moment while I go and check the list of available courses. We may have cross referenced the entries.' Her finger hovered over one of the items. 'Yes, I'll do that. I'll be back in a couple of minutes.' She didn't say any more, but turned the book half way towards them, tapping her finger in what appeared to be an absent-minded fashion in the same place as before. Then she walked away, disappearing into a nearby office.

Lewis smiled. He glanced at Kayleigh and

then pointed a finger at the place on the page that the woman had seemed to indicate.

'It looks very much as though we've found what we're looking for, doesn't it? Isn't that your sister's name written there, alongside her home address? There's even the name of the company she's working for just now, and a phone number so that she might be reached in the daytime.'

Kayleigh was busy memorising the details. 'You think the clerk meant for us to see that?'

'Oh, yes. I do.'

The clerk came back a short time later, saying, 'I've had a look at the list of secretarial courses that we do here, but so far I haven't found anything that might help you. I'm afraid I don't know what more I can do.'

'That's all right,' Lewis said. 'You've been very helpful.'

Kayleigh echoed that. 'Thank you so much for your time and trouble.'

'You're welcome.'

They went back to the car, and Kayleigh tried to contain her excitement. 'It feels as though we're really close to finding her,' she said.

Lewis nodded. 'From the address, it looks as though she's living nearby. We'll head over there right now...but she might not be at home, you know. It's possible that she'll be at work.'

'An estate agent's office, wasn't it? Yes, you could be right.'

It didn't take them long to find the house. Some half an hour later they stepped out of the car and walked along a row of terraced properties, situated in an older part of the town. Heather's house was some way along the terrace. There wasn't any sign of movement inside, and when they knocked on the door no one came to answer.

A neighbour opened her door. She was in her thirties, dark-haired, with a friendly, open expression. 'Are you looking for someone?' she asked. 'Can I help you?' A small child peered out from behind her skirt, and she stroked the little girl's head, as though to reassure her.

'Thank you...yes. I'm looking for my sister,' Kayleigh explained. She drew a photograph from her bag and showed it to the woman. 'I wasn't sure whether she was living around here.'

The woman studied the picture. 'That's

Heather,' she said. 'She's at work just now, but she should be back home in about half an hour.' She looked carefully at Kayleigh. 'Actually, she looks a bit like you. I take it she's not expecting you? You haven't phoned, or anything?'

Kayleigh shook her head, but Lewis said quietly, 'We were hoping that it would be something of a surprise…a nice one, of course.'

The neighbour took that on board. 'Yes, I expect it will be. She talks about her sister from time to time…about the things they used to do, the places they would visit.' She glanced from one to the other. 'Do you want to come in and wait for her?'

Kayleigh shook her head. 'No…thank you. I think I'll go for a walk and come back a little later. It was good of you to offer.' She needed to get her head together and she didn't think she could do that in someone else's house. She felt restless, as though she needed to keep on the move.

Lewis seemed to understand. As the woman closed the door and they started to walk away, he said, 'There's a small park back along the way we came. I noticed it when we drove down here. It's just a couple of streets away. Do you want to go and sit there for a while?'

'Yes, that would be good.' She was bubbling over with barely suppressed excitement, but she was racked with nervous apprehension at the same time. As they walked, she was trying hard to contain her fears.

'What will I do if she doesn't want to come back home with me? Aunt Jane is pinning her hopes on seeing her again. What if she doesn't want to know us?'

By now they had reached the park, and they went through the gates and headed for a grassed area that was shaded by silver birch trees. The sunlight was dappled here, and it was quiet, away from the main thoroughfare and reasonably secluded. In the distance, children were playing on a segment of land that had been set aside for climbing frames and swings, but here there were only the birds to disturb the tranquillity.

'You heard what the neighbour said…she's been talking about you. That has to mean that she still cares, doesn't it?'

'Not necessarily. After all, if we were so close, why didn't she turn to me for help? Why did she leave in the first place?' She ran her palm over his shirtsleeve, her fingers closing lightly

around his arm, as though she needed his close-
ness to invigorate her, give her the courage she
was lacking.

'You'll have the answers to all those questions soon enough,' he said, a smile playing
around his mouth. 'I'm sure your sister will be
glad to see you.'

She stared up at him, anguish in her grey eyes.
'But you said…before, you said…'

'Forget what I said. It doesn't matter now.
You're here. You're going to meet up with her
in a little while.' He looked down at her, letting
his gaze travel slowly over her stricken features.
'You've waited for this for a long time.'

'Yes, but—'

She didn't get to say any more because he cut
her off, the words lost as his head came down
and his mouth claimed hers. The kiss took her
breath away and swept everything out of her
mind…everything, except for the sheer joy of
having him kiss her, his lips tasting hers, his
hands smoothing over her body as though he
would explore every curve.

'Hmm…you feel so good. I could get used to
this.' He murmured the words against her cheek,

and Kayleigh echoed the sentiment. There was something special about being held in his arms. As though he read her thoughts, he drew her against him, and her limbs melted as the long line of his taut thighs pressured hers, and her soft breasts were crushed against the solid wall of his chest.

'You can't imagine how long I've wanted to do this.' His words were a warm breath against her cheek, and a tremor of excitement ran through her as his lips went on an excursion, tracing the line of her jaw, gliding downwards to explore the silken column of her throat.

His hands shaped her, leaving a trail of ecstasy as his thumb brushed the soft swell of her breast. The nub tautened in response, and a delicious ache started up inside her, shimmering through her body in a rippling motion. This felt so good, so right, and she wanted it to go on for ever.

She looked up at him. Perhaps she had said it aloud, because his blue gaze meshed with hers, a teasing, amused glitter lighting up his eyes as he drank in her rapt expression. He knew exactly what his touch was doing to her, and perhaps that had been his aim all along. He wanted her to forget what she was about, to calm her nerves and give her something else to focus her attention on.

Well, he had succeeded. She wanted nothing more than to stay here, wrapped up in his arms, safe from the hazards of every day life and plunged into a world of sweet, thrilling rapture.

His fingers swept upwards, caressing the nape of her neck and tangling playfully with her silk-soft curls. He said huskily, 'You're beautiful, Kayleigh, so lovely, and I wish that I could stay here like this and make love to you for a long, long time.'

'I didn't realise that anything could feel so good,' she whispered against his chest. 'But you're right...we have to go. I can't miss this chance to see my sister after all this time.'

Reluctantly, she eased herself away from him. Her heart was still hammering, taking more than a little while to settle down. She said huskily, 'Shall we go?'

He nodded, and together they walked back to the house, both of them experiencing a close-ness that hadn't been there before. Was there just a chance that this sometimes remote man might be at last coming to see how good life could be when he shared his feelings with her?

They arrived back at the terraced block just as a young woman was putting her key in the lock. The woman had chestnut-coloured hair, cut in a youthful style, with curls framing her face.

Kayleigh held her breath, and Lewis asked quietly, 'Is that your sister?'

Kayleigh nodded, unable to speak because her throat was suddenly tight.

'You should go and speak to her.'

He stopped walking and hung back, so that Kayleigh turned to him and said, 'Come with me?'

He shook his head. 'No…I'll wait for you. I'll take a walk, but you can ring me and let me know when you're ready for me to fetch you.'

She hadn't expected him to say that, but her sister was opening the door, and Kayleigh wanted to talk to her before she went inside. She hurried over to her, calling her name, and Heather stood very still, turning a little, her eyes widening with stunned surprise.

'Kayleigh?'

'Yes.' She held out her arms to her sister, and the two girls hugged one another, three years dropping away as though they had never been apart. 'I'm so glad I found you. I brought someone with me, a friend, someone very special to me...' She turned to include Lewis in the get-together, but he had gone, and her heart plummeted like a stone.

Heather said, 'I have to go and fetch Anne-Marie from next door. Just give me a minute and we'll go into the house.' Her mouth made an awkward shape. 'We have a lot of catching up to do.'

Kayleigh pulled in a sharp breath. She didn't know why her sister had to go next door, but the name Anne-Marie was familiar, and just a little while later, when Heather reappeared with the little girl that Kayleigh had seen earlier, everything fell into place.

'She's your little girl, isn't she?' she asked softly as they went into Heather's house. The child was about two and a half years old, a sweet little girl, with chestnut hair and grey eyes that reflected her mother's solemn expression.

'Yes. I named her after Mum.' Her eyes

clouded. 'I was so sorry about leaving her. That was my biggest regret, next to leaving you. Did she get my postcards?'

'Yes, she did. They made her happy and sad all the same time, because she desperately wanted to see you again.'

Heather lowered her head. 'I heard that she had died, and I felt awful about it. Someone showed me a newspaper, and I read a piece about it. The paper was out of date, and it was too late for me to come back by then. Besides, I wasn't sure whether or not Evan would still be around. I could imagine him lording it all over the place.'

'He isn't there any more. We saw him off, me and Aunt Jane…with a little help from our friend next door.'

'He's the man who was with you just now?' Kayleigh nodded, and Heather smiled. 'I only caught a glimpse of him, but he's dishy.'

They giggled, and suddenly it was like old times. Anne-Marie lost some of her shyness, and came towards Kayleigh. 'I done a picture,' she said. 'I done it with paints, and then I put some sparkle on it.'

Kayleigh admired the painting that the child held out. 'That is so beautiful,' she said.

Pleased, Anne-Marie went to rummage in a box, and found a teddy bear. She sat down by the box and danced the bear on the rug, starting to tell him the story of her day.

Kayleigh said softly, 'Is she Jacob's child?'

Heather nodded, and Kayleigh asked, 'Is she the reason why you went away, and stayed away?'

'Yes.' The words came out almost as a whisper. 'That, and I couldn't cope with Evan and his temper any longer. I could imagine him raising the roof if he knew that I was going to have a child. He had enough to say about everything else.'

'He's not going to be a problem, any longer. He threatened to see me in court, but the solicitor wrote and told him that he had no claims once the divorce settlement came through and he accepted it.'

'There was a divorce?' Heather's eyes widened.

Kayleigh nodded. 'Mum started proceedings before she died.'

Heather was silent, taking that in, and Kayleigh glanced at the little girl, saying under her breath after a while, 'Don't you think you should let Jacob know about her?'

'No.' The answer was vehement, but then Heather added on a calmer note, 'I don't want him to know. He mustn't find out about her. That's partly why I stayed away for so long. He would have asked questions, and nothing would have gone the way I wanted.'

Kayleigh stayed with Heather for some time, finding out about how she had looked after herself these last three years, and about her plans for the future. She tried to persuade her to come home with her, but Heather was adamant that she wouldn't do that. In the end, Kayleigh realised that her efforts were coming to no good, and that it wouldn't be fair to keep Lewis waiting any longer.

'I shall have to go,' she said. 'Will you promise me that you won't disappear again? I couldn't bear it if I was to lose you all over again. You will keep in touch with me, won't you?'

Heather nodded, and a little while later they said goodbye to one another. Kayleigh hugged her sister and gave the little girl a kiss, and then went in search of Lewis.

He met her at the place where they had left the car earlier. He must have seen that she was subdued, because he didn't say very much as they began the journey back to Devon, and Kayleigh limited herself to telling him the basics, that Heather had a little girl and that she was renting the house on a temporary basis while she found her feet.

Eventually, when they were about halfway home, he said, 'I can imagine that you must have tried to persuade her to come back with you. Did she tell you what the problem was?'

'She said that Jacob didn't want a family. He had told her that he wasn't ready to have children, and he thought she was too young to settle down. She thought that if she had stayed at home and had the baby, they would have been pressured into getting married, or that Jacob would have thought it would be the right thing to do. Knowing how he felt about things, she didn't want that. She thought it would be better if he didn't know about the baby.'

Kayleigh grimaced. 'Besides, Evan would have made her life miserable if she had stayed on as a single parent. She had the feeling that even if she had found a place of her own nearer home, he would have tried to make her feel like an outcast. I think Mum tried to smooth things over whenever there were arguments, but she didn't win very often. That's when she started to see him for what he really was.'

She sighed. 'And as to Jacob, the last time Heather saw him they had a terrific argument. It all blew up over nothing, but she wasn't in the best frame of mind, and he made it clear that the last thing he wanted to do was to move in with her. I suppose she wasn't thinking straight, and when a friend offered her a place to stay, she took off. Perhaps it was the pregnancy hormones that threw her a little off kilter. She said she needed to go away to get her head straight, but the longer she stayed away, the more difficult it was for her to come back.'

Lewis turned the car on to the coast road. 'I think I can understand how Jacob might have been wary of setting up home together with your sister. He seems to have his own issues with staying independent. And if it's true that he didn't want children, then I could see that there would have been problems in the relationship right from the start. Even so, I dare say he might have felt duty-bound to do the right thing by her.'

Kayleigh felt a surge of annoyance rising inside her. 'If he didn't want children, then he should have acted in a responsible manner from the outset.'

'That's true, but life doesn't always work out that way, does it?'

Kayleigh scowled at him. She might have known that he would identify with Jacob's point of view.

'You would side with him. Why should either of you even consider looking at things from a woman's point of view? They're irrelevant, you're both quite happy to go on living your solitary existence. It suits you to be that way. You don't need anyone, and you don't want children cluttering up your life. That would be too much like taking on family responsibility, wouldn't it?'

He pressed his lips together. 'That sounds like a fair summing-up,' he said.

He didn't elaborate on that, and Kayleigh simmered for a while longer. 'Doesn't it ever occur to you that your experience of family life was very unusual, and that it has coloured your judgement ever since? Perhaps you're afraid to dip your toes in the water.'

'I'm not afraid. I just don't see why I should burden myself with the trappings of family life when they mean nothing to me.'

Kayleigh slipped into silence for the rest of the journey. There was no hope for him. When he had kissed her, she had been lulled into a false sense of security. She had dared to think that he might want her and need her, but that was just an illusion.

CHAPTER TEN

'WHERE are you, Aunt Jane?' Kayleigh walked through the rooms of the house, going in search of her aunt. She was bursting to tell her the news, that she had actually been talking to Heather, but her aunt was nowhere to be seen. The rooms were empty.

Margaret came in from the garden just as Kayleigh was going to take a look upstairs. Her face was ashen, and she looked drained and near to tears. 'You're back,' she said. 'I thought I heard the car draw up.'

'Yes...Lewis just dropped me off.' He had gone to his own place, saying that he had work to do, and because she was still grappling with his reaction to Heather's predicament, Kayleigh hadn't put up any objections, and she hadn't invited him in for coffee. Perhaps that had been a mistake, after he had been good enough to go with her today, but he, too, had appeared to be in an odd frame of mind.

She frowned, taking in Margaret's expression. 'What's wrong? What's happened?'

'I didn't know what to do for the best,' Margaret said. She looked as though she was shaking. 'Your aunt was taken ill a couple of hours ago and I had to call for an ambulance to take her to the hospital. I've just come back from there. They say they're going to keep her in.'

Kayleigh let out a shocked gasp. 'What's wrong with her? Is it the heart rhythm again? I thought we had that more or less under control now. We spoke to Mr Morrison, the consultant, and he sorted things out with Dr Havers.'

'I don't know.' Margaret started wringing her hands. 'I don't think it's that. She was in such a lot of pain…it was her abdomen, I think. She was vomiting, and I didn't know what to do for the best. I'm just so worried about her. They say they have to do tests.'

She was pacing the floor. 'I thought about calling you, but I knew how much it meant to you, going to find your sister, and I knew that it wouldn't be all that long before you were home. There wasn't any point dragging you all the way back here. You would only have been worried, and I was afraid that you might get into an accident or something if you were to come rushing back.'

'It's all right, Margaret.' Kayleigh was trying to stem her own feelings of anxiety. 'You don't need to blame yourself for anything. I'm really grateful to you for looking after my aunt, and you've been such a good friend to her over the last few weeks. I'm going to go over to the hospital right now to see how she's doing, and I'll ring you and let you know what's happening.' She glanced at her neighbour. 'You look worn out…perhaps you should go home and try to get some rest. This must have been such a shock for you.'

Margaret nodded. 'Yes, it has knocked all the stuffing out of me, I think.'

Kayleigh saw her back to her own house before hurrying to get herself ready for the journey to the hospital. She had no idea what was going on, but she packed a few clothes and toiletries that she thought her aunt might need.

When she arrived at the hospital, she found that her aunt was in a bad way. Through a glass panel in the door Kayleigh could see that she was lying on a bed, unmoving, connected up to a cardiac monitor. There was an intravenous line in her arm so that the medical team could give her fluids and medication. She was breathing oxygen through a mask.

'Do the doctors have any idea what might be wrong with her?' Kayleigh asked the nurse who was checking the monitors.

'They're not sure whether it might be pancreatitis or some form of colitis,' the nurse said.

Kayleigh's brows met in a straight line. 'She's never had any trouble of that sort before…but perhaps I'll have a chance to talk to the doctor about it later.' She sent the nurse a swift look. 'Do you think I might go and sit with her?'

'Yes, I should think that would be all right, for a little while at least. Her pain was very severe so we have her on morphine at the moment. She might be able to say a few words, but don't expect very much more. She asked for you, and then she asked for Dr McAllister. She seemed anxious to see him for some reason, so we gave him a call.'

Kayleigh frowned at that, but she didn't waste any more time on wondering about it and she hurried to her aunt's bedside and gently clasped her hand.

'Did you see her?' Aunt Jane's voice was thready.

'Heather? Yes, I did. She's all right, and she's going to keep in touch.' She didn't think it would be wise to burden her aunt with any more than that right now, and her aunt simply attempted a smile and then closed her eyes.

Kayleigh was desperately worried. Somehow she didn't think her aunt was suffering from either of the conditions the nurse had mentioned. She could see, though, that her aunt was very ill, and it was upsetting to feel that she could do nothing to help her.

A few minutes later, Lewis came quietly into the room. 'How is she?' he asked in a hushed voice. His expression was sombre.

Kayleigh shook her head. 'Not good.'

He went over to the bedside and looked down at Aunt Jane. Her face was pale, but she appeared to have a slight fever, with tiny beads of perspiration breaking out on her forehead.

'I can't believe that she was up and about just this morning,' Lewis said, keeping his voice low. He looked as though he was utterly shocked by the gravity of her situation.

Aunt Jane had appeared to be sleeping, but she must have somehow been alerted to Lewis's presence because she opened her eyes and gave him a gentle smile. He moved closer and lightly stroked her hand, and Kayleigh felt a lump come up in her throat at the exchange of affection she saw pass between them.

'I'm glad that you're here,' Aunt Jane said, and he had to strain to hear her words. 'I want you to promise me that you'll take care of Kayleigh.'

Lewis's eyes widened. 'Jane, you sound as though you're giving up.' He shook his head. 'You mustn't do that. You're going to get well.'

Aunt Jane clasped his hand, a determined light flickering in her eyes. 'Promise me,' she said.

'I promise.' He shook his head. 'But it won't be necessary for me to do that. We're going to make you well again. I'm going to talk to the doctors, and we'll get you back on your feet again. You have to believe that.'

Aunt Jane closed her eyes and appeared to drift off into sleep. The nurse came to check her medication once more and said quietly, 'I think you should both leave now. She needs to rest.'

Reluctantly, Kayleigh stood up to go. Lewis followed her out of the room, his face set in grim lines, and he said through tight lips, 'Why didn't you call me to tell me that she had been rushed to hospital?'

'Why would you need to know about it?' Kayleigh answered, her manner equally blunt and abrasive. 'Haven't you told me enough times that families don't mean anything to you...that you don't need anyone?'

His head went back at that as though she had struck him in the face. 'But this is different. This is Jane... You know how well we get on with one another...you should have told me that she was ill.'

'I don't see the difference,' Kayleigh said, shrugging. 'Heather and Jacob used to get along very well, and now they have a child, but you can't see any reason why they should have stayed in touch with one another. Isn't it all part and parcel of the same thing? We either care about people, or we don't. I don't see that there are any half-measures.'

He was frowning now, and he said in an edgy tone, 'I was speaking generally. I wasn't implying that a man shouldn't acknowledge his own child.'

'Weren't you? That was the impression I had.'

He stared at her. 'Then you were wrong. Anyway, we're wasting time,' he said, his mouth straightening. 'Instead of arguing pointlessly with one another, we should be doing all that we can to help get your aunt on the mend.' He frowned. 'I heard that they were going to do a CT scan and some more lab tests—I think we need more than that. That kind of approach to diagnosis is far too leisurely and time-consuming. We need to take more aggressive measures.'

'What are you suggesting?'

'I think we should get in touch with a vascular surgeon. To my mind, it can't be unrelated that she's been suffering from atrial fibrillation, but I don't think we're going to be able to sort this one out unless we do an angiogram. That would show up any blockage in the artery, and it needs to be done right away.'

'So you think this has something to do with the arrhythmia?'

'I do. The problem with a heart that beats in a chaotic fashion is that people are liable to suffer from blood clots as a result, or it may be that an embolism breaks off and causes a blockage. It's possible that this is what's happened in Jane's case, and that's why she was in such pain. I have a horrible feeling that if she doesn't go for surgery very soon the outlook is bleak.'

Kayleigh was worried. 'Will you speak to the consultant in charge? Your voice will carry much more weight than mine.'

He nodded. He was already walking off in the direction of the nurses' station and once there he reached for the phone.

Things started to happen very quickly after that. Her aunt was whisked away for diagnostic testing, the vascular surgeon was called, and within the hour she was in Theatre, undergoing surgery.

Kayleigh waited with Lewis in his office down in A and E.

'Have you told your sister what's happening?' he asked.

'Yes, I rang her. She was upset, and she said that

she'll come over as soon as she can get a baby-sitter. I told her that she could bring Anne-Marie with her, and we'll look after her at home, but I don't know whether she'll do that. She's worried that she might run into Jacob at some point.'

Lewis busied himself making coffee in the filter machine. 'That's always possible, of course, but the alternative is that she spends the rest of her life running away.'

He went on cautiously, 'The house belongs to both of you now, doesn't it? Did you mention to your sister the possibility of selling up? After all, now that you know where she is, it means that you don't have to keep your own life on hold any longer. You were talking at one time about moving out, weren't you...if only for your aunt's sake, so that she doesn't have the hills to climb, and so that you could find a house that's easier to manage?'

'That's right. It did come up in conversation...in passing... but we haven't decided anything yet. These are early days, and we still have to get used to the fact that we've found each other.'

Kayleigh made a wry face. 'I went out to look

at the barn conversion the other day, because I saw that there was a for-sale sign up. I made a few enquiries with the estate agent...just out of curiosity, really...and it seems that they've had lots of interest in the place. They have a prospective buyer who had come over from France, and he's very keen on getting the property. They seem to think it's almost a done deal, so I guess that puts me out of the picture, even if I was in a position to put in an offer...which I'm not.'

They drank coffee and Kayleigh tried not to dwell on the things that weren't to be. Her priority now had to be Aunt Jane, and that pushed everything into the background...everything except for Lewis.

She didn't know what to make of him. He always seemed so very much in command of himself, and yet for just a moment back there, when he had let his guard down, she had glimpsed his utter devastation at the thought that they might lose Aunt Jane.

About an hour later the office door was pushed open, and the surgeon came in to talk to them. 'I've just come from completing the surgery on your aunt,' he said. 'I don't think I'd be wrong in saying that if she had been left in that condition any longer, she might not have survived. The angiogram showed an arterial occlusion, but I've managed to remove the embolism that was causing the trouble. I'm hopeful that we've managed to deal with the situation, and I believe your aunt should make a good recovery. It'll take a while, mind, but I think she'll be all right.'

Kayleigh let out a sigh of relief. 'That's wonderful news. Thank you so much.'

Lewis thanked him as well, and he left the room with the surgeon after a few minutes, talking to him about the extent of the operation. Kayleigh went to find her aunt, preparing to sit with her until she was well enough to be able to talk.

Over the next few days, while her aunt was in hospital, Kayleigh took time out to go and visit her whenever she was on a break, and Lewis did the same.

'Things are turning out better than I expected,' he said, meeting up with Kayleigh in the corridor outside Aunt Jane's room. 'Jane is doing really well, and I just had news that the little girl that we brought in from the cliff fall is making a good recovery.'

'Is she? I asked the receptionist to let me know what was happening, but I haven't seen her yet this afternoon. That's brilliant news.'

When the day came for her aunt to be discharged, Lewis was there to help her settle into the car for the journey home.

'I want you to come back to the house,' Aunt Jane said, looking up at him. 'Kayleigh said that she was putting on a bit of a spread, a few nibbles, sandwiches, and cake and so on, and she said that Heather would be there, with her little girl. You will come, won't you? It wouldn't be right without you.'

'She told me about it, and I'll be there,' he told her. 'I'm going off duty in a few minutes, so I'll come and join you as soon as I can.' He frowned. 'I'm not sure that you should be getting all excited, though, and turning into a party animal as soon as you get back home. Next thing, you'll be boogying out on the terrace.'

Aunt Jane laughed. 'That's all your fault,' she said. 'You bring out the girl in me. If I was just thirty years younger, you'd have to watch out.'

Kayleigh opened the door to him some half an hour later. 'We're in the sitting room,' she said. 'I've opened out the doors from the dining room, so we can wander through and help ourselves to food.'

They walked along the hallway. 'It isn't really a get-together,' she explained. 'It's just Heather and Anne-Marie, but Aunt Jane only saw them once while she was in the hospital, and I know she was looking forward to seeing them again. This seemed like the best way of making it happen.'

'It sounds like a good idea,' he agreed. 'Jane's doing really well, isn't she? Considering all that she's been through, she's come out of this with flying colours.'

'I'm just glad that everything turned out the way it did. It was all such a shock, and I'm only just coming back down to earth.' She looked at him. 'You know, I can't help thinking that it's all because of you that she's still here with us. I never did thank you for that, did I? If you hadn't started things moving when you did, she might never have gone for surgery, and we probably wouldn't be welcoming her back home now.'

He tilted his head a fraction to one side, looking at her, a smile playing around his mouth. 'I don't need any thanks,' he said, 'but if you insist...I can think of a perfect way for you to do that.' He was teasing her, but his hands were already sliding around her waist, tugging her to him, and she would have gone into his arms willingly, gladly, except that the doorbell rang just then.

She frowned. 'I wonder who that can be? I'm not expecting anyone else.' He released her and she went to answer it, and as she pulled the door open she saw that it was Jacob who was standing there.

She stared at him for a moment, until she managed at last to get herself together, and then she said, 'Come in, Jacob. It's good to see you.' A line etched its way into her brow. 'I had no idea that you were going to be in the area.' At the same time, she was wondering how she was going to deal with the fact that Heather and Anne-Marie were both in the sitting room.

Jacob glanced awkwardly at Lewis, and there was something in the look that passed between them that made her instantly suspicious.

'Do you know something about this?' she said, looking at Lewis.

He didn't try to deny it. 'I gave him a call, on the off-chance that he might drop by. I doubt that it will be as awkward a situation as you think,' he said. 'I put Heather and Jacob in touch with one another a while ago, after we came back from Cornwall. I thought perhaps they could manage to sort things out between them, once one of them had plucked up enough courage to make the first move. Jacob decided that he could be the one to do that.'

Jacob had the grace to look sheepish. 'Lewis helped me to think things through...and I suppose, deep down, I've known all along that I must have had a lot to do with Heather's decision to go away in the first place. I thought the least I could do was to go and talk to her.'

He winced. 'Things are still a little fragile between us, so that's perhaps why she hasn't mentioned anything to you about what's going on. I think she had the wrong idea about how I felt. I always wanted to be with her, but I thought perhaps we would have some time to ourselves before we thought about starting a family. I didn't have any idea that she was already pregnant…and, of course, that changes everything.'

Kayleigh looked at him steadily, her mouth taking on a slightly fractious look. She wasn't best pleased with Lewis for intervening this way without telling her what he was planning on doing. It wasn't what Heather had wanted, but it was too late to complain about that now.

'I think you should be telling all this to Heather, not to me, don't you agree? You'll find her in the sitting room.' She waved her hand in the direction of the room, and Jacob started towards it. Lewis followed before she had a chance to waylay him and demand an explanation.

Heather seemed to be taken completely by surprise when Jacob walked into the room. She coloured up, and for a moment it looked as though she didn't know what to do.

Anne-Marie had no such qualms. She ran up to Jacob and flung her arms around him. 'I seed you before, didn't I?' she said. 'You bringed me a dolly.'

'That's right, sweetheart.' Jacob smiled down

at the little girl, his gaze filled with pride and affection as he bent to give her a hug. 'I can see that you brought the dolly with you today. I'm glad that you like her. She was a special gift for my own sweet little girl.'

By now Heather had recovered enough to find her voice. 'She takes her doll everywhere with her. I think you've won her over. She talks about you all the time.' She gave him a rueful look.

Aunt Jane looked from one to the other and said, 'At last. It's about time you two started to talk to one another and make sense of things, instead of making a big shambles out of everything.'

Then she turned her attention to Lewis, and had him fill up a plate with food and come and sit next to her. She wasn't eating very much herself, but she looked so much better than she had before, and Kayleigh was relieved about that.

All her plans had been thrown upside down, with Jacob turning up this way. It could well have ended in disaster, but instead things seemed to be turning out much better than she could ever have imagined.

After they had finished eating, Heather and Jacob went to sit on the sofa, side by side, looking through old family photographs and fetching up memories, and Aunt Jane was adding her two-pennyworth. There was a lot of good humour and friendly banter, but after a while it occurred to Kayleigh that Lewis wasn't joining in. He had that far-away look in his eyes that she had seen before, and his mouth was straight, his jaw set in a rigid manner.

'I should go,' he said, a few minutes later, and mumbled something about having things to do. He slipped out of the door and had started along the hallway before Kayleigh actually realised that he was leaving.

'Go after him, love,' Aunt Jane said. 'We'll be all right here.'

Kayleigh made a brief, frozen kind of smile and headed after him. She might have known that her aunt wouldn't have missed anything. For all that she made light of things, she seemed to know exactly what was going on.

She followed him back to his own house, catching up with him as he was opening his back door. 'You shot off so fast that I didn't know what was happening,' she said. 'Can I come in and talk to you?'

He seemed to hesitate, but then said, 'Of course.' He glanced down at her feet. 'Just make sure the cat doesn't trip you up.'

The grey cat was arching his back, sinuously curving himself around her legs and making a sound of satisfaction. Kayleigh smiled down at him, stroking his soft fur. 'You like being fussed over, don't you?' she said.

'He certainly seems to have taken to you.' Lewis pushed open the kitchen door and snapped on the light. 'We'll go through to the sitting room, if you like. It's the most comfortable room, now that the decorating is finished.'

She went with him into the room. 'It's lovely…' she murmured. 'All clean and fresh. The furnishings are perfect, soft and smooth and just right for the room. I don't remember seeing them before.'

'I bought new covers,' he said, his tone flat. 'John will be coming home soon, and I thought I ought to make an effort to get things finished. Go and try out the sofa…it's comfy.'

She did as he suggested, and as he continued to wander about the room she said quietly, 'What made you leave so suddenly? Had you had enough of hearing us all chatter? I suppose we're a bit mundane…nothing much happens to shake us up and family photos are only interesting to those who took part, I suppose.'

'No, it was good. You were all getting along really well, and it was something special to see you all looking so contented. I'm the one who has the problem. I just don't fit in. I don't belong.'

She stood up and went over to him. 'That's not true. We all wanted you to be there.'

He grimaced. 'Perhaps…but I'm an outsider. I'm not used to these sorts of occasions and, to be honest, it's better if I stay away. I don't really feel comfortable in those situations. I don't fit in. I would probably end up doing or saying the wrong thing.'

She studied him for a long moment. There was tension in the way he moved his mouth, and a muscle flicked faintly along the line of his jaw. She said carefully, 'So because you don't fit in, you've decided that you're going to stay an outsider and live the rest of your life in the shadows, are you?'

He stared at her. 'I don't know what you mean.'

'Are you sure about that?' She saw the way he held his shoulders back, how his head lifted and his eyes had that remote look that she was coming to know so well. 'I think you're afraid of being hurt, the way you were when you were a child. You never felt as though you belonged anywhere, and now you think it's the norm, so you isolate yourself before you can be sucked in. Backing away has become like an automatic mode of self-defence…it's instinctive.'

His mouth made a crooked twist. 'Since when did you become a psychiatrist?'

'See? There you go again.' Her grey eyes challenged him. 'If you can't win the argument, you hit out. But you've come unstuck this time, because I'm not backing off. We love you and we care about you, and you're part of our family, our wider family, whether you like it or not.'

'You know that's not true.' He shook his head. 'Families are flesh and blood, and even those ties don't always bind.'

'Maybe not, but does that mean adopted children aren't loved, that parents who adopt aren't capable of making a loving home? The thing is, Lewis, I saw your expression when you thought we might lose my aunt, and that told me more than anything that you can share those loving emotions with the rest of us. You may try to fob us off and deny it, but I've seen it with my own eyes. You care about her just as much as the rest of us...and she cares about you, so that means you have every right to share our family get-togethers.'

'Maybe. I don't know.'

Kayleigh reached out to him and tentatively ran her fingers over his arms. Part of her was afraid that he would reject her all over again, but her heart was telling her that she had to take that chance.

'It's taken me a long time,' she said, 'but I think I'm finally beginning to understand the real you, the man that you try to keep hidden away inside yourself.' She smiled up at him. 'You said that you understood how Jacob might want to keep his independence, and yet you told him where Heather was living and you talked to him so that he would think about what he needed to do. That doesn't come from a man who doesn't care about people.'

He frowned. 'I never said that I didn't care. I took up medicine because I need to be able to do some good for others, and I want to be able to help people.'

'But it isn't enough, is it?' She held on to him when he might have turned away. 'You're coming to the point where you see that other people live their lives differently, and you can't go on denying that you want a part of that warmth and humanity.'

He grimaced. 'Things don't always work out the way we want them to.'

'Perhaps not…but in your case, it might be that you can't move on until you've faced up to the problem of your childhood. It's like a blast of frozen air that forms icicles that dig into you and spike all your plans.'

'How am I supposed to deal with that? It's past and gone.'

She shook her head. 'I don't think it is. Your parents are still around, and you could make contact with them. You could tell them how you feel, and ask if they ever thought about what they were doing and what effect it would have on you. Perhaps they thought they were building the foundations of a good life and lost their way somehow.'

His jaw flexed. 'You said that once before, that I should talk to them.'

He moved, and she thought perhaps she had gone too far and that he was going to brush her off once again, but instead he lifted a hand and let his fingers trail amongst the softness of her hair. 'Let's just imagine for a moment that you could be right,' he said, 'and I have all this tension locked up inside me. How is it that you seem to know so much about me, about the way I think?'

His blue gaze wandered over her face and for a second or two her mouth wavered. 'Because I've been watching you,' she said huskily. 'I can't help myself...I love you.' Loving him was part of her now. She had come to realise it, and now, at last, she had stopped fighting the emotion.

She waited for his reaction, but he did nothing. He was very still, the fingers that had been lightly stroking her hair became motionless, so that his palm rested warmly against her head. Then he closed his eyes, as though he was absorbing her words into himself.

After a moment or two he looked at her and said softly, 'Are you sure that's how you feel?'

She nodded, and he asked, 'How do you know that it's real? Perhaps you're confusing what you feel with compassion and sadness for the child who was lost.'

'I don't think so. You see, I've come to realise that I love you in spite of yourself. I've seen you when you're moody and sharp and when you want to be left alone to work through your irritability, when most people would stay away. But I know that there's another side to you, as well…the part of you that reaches out to help people, that shows care and consideration and understanding. I love you for who you are, not for who you were or might become.'

He gently drew her to him, his hand warm at the nape of her neck, and then he laid a tender kiss on her brow. She tilted her head back so that she could look up at him, and he followed through, claiming her mouth with a kiss that was passionate and exhilarating at the same time. The blood rocketed through her veins, surging through her body from head to toe, until she swayed with sheer, pulsating excitement and he held her in his arms, caressing her, throwing her senses into hectic disarray.

'I love you, too,' he murmured against her lips. 'I've been telling myself that it couldn't be, that you would never want someone like me…I tried to shake it off and make it stop, because I was afraid that it would all go wrong.'

He gazed down at her, his hands stroking the curve of her hips, shifting to shape the length of her spine. 'I need this to be right. I love you, but I don't know if I can make you happy. I'm afraid that it might all blow up in my face.'

She lifted her hand to his face and let her fingers explore the contours of his cheek. 'No one can tell what the future holds,' she said. 'We all live in fear that things will go wrong…but if we don't follow our hearts we'll never know what might have been.' She smiled up at him, her gaze tender and loving. 'All I know is that you're the best thing that's happened to me in a long, long time, and I know, deep inside, that we can make this work. For me, loving you will last a lifetime.'

He kissed her again, holding her close, and after a while he said, 'I won't let you down. I won't be the one to cast this love aside.'

'Then we'll be together for always.' She

nestled her head against his chest, her arms around him, feeling the thud of his heart beneath her cheek.

He drew in a deep breath. 'Will you marry me, Kayleigh?' he murmured, his voice roughened. 'I want to do this properly. It has to be right.'

She looked up at him. 'Yes, I will.' A mischievous smile crossed her mouth. 'Of course, that means you'll have to leave John to his own devices and start thinking about living somewhere else.'

'That's true.' He gave her a thoughtful glance. 'But it works both ways. Do you think you'll want to stay at the house next door or will you want to find somewhere else?'

She wrinkled her nose. 'The only place I've wanted to live is the barn conversion, but the sold notice went up the other day, so that's my dream house off the list.'

'Hmm…that's not necessarily true.'

'Why isn't it? What do you mean?'

His mouth made a crooked slant. 'Well, in fact, I was the one who bought it. I stepped in with the full asking price and offered a cash deal, so they almost snatched my hand off.'

Her eyes widened. 'It's yours?' She thought about that for a moment. 'Had you already decided to move out of this place?'

'Sort of.' He ran his palm lightly over her shoulder and down her arm. 'I knew that you wanted it, and I could see that someone was ready to make an offer, so I thought I might take a chance and secure it for you. I knew it would be ideal... there's even a granny annexe which would be just right for Jane.'

She stood on tiptoe and kissed him hard on the mouth. 'I knew there was a reason why I love you. I love you, I love you, I love you...'

He laughed and started to rain kisses all over her face. 'Ditto, ditto, ditto...'

After a while, when she had recovered herself, she said curiously, 'You said that you paid cash to clinch the deal—that must have taken some doing, even for a consultant. Have you been saving up or something?'

'Or something. My father may have cut me off, but my grandparents left me an inheritance that will keep me going for life. They were lovely people, my gran and grandad. They saw me through the bad times, and they encouraged me to follow my instincts and take up medicine. I miss them. I would sooner have them here, and lose the inheritance, but at least it bought the barn conversion, so that's some consolation.'

Kayleigh let out a long breath and wondered how she could comfort him. She said slowly, 'They lived good, long lives, didn't they?'

'Yes, that's true...that's something to be thankful for.'

She started to open her mouth to say something, and he said, 'I know what you're thinking. You're going to ask me to get in touch with my parents, aren't you?'

She nodded. 'Will you...if only to talk things through and bring about some kind of closure?'

'Yes, if it will make you happy.' He winced. 'Besides, we both have to get to know them if we're going to invite them to the wedding.'

She chuckled. 'Shall we go and tell the others next door? I can't wait to see Aunt Jane's face. She loves you to bits, you know.'

His mouth curved. 'I think she probably already knows how this is going to turn out. Didn't you notice how she set us up to be with one another at the hospital?'

Kayleigh gave a soft laugh. 'That's my aunt.' She wound her arms around his neck and tilted her face to him. 'We'll go and tell them in a little while, shall we?'

'Definitely. In a little while.' He lowered his head and kissed her tenderly, until both of them forgot all about the passing of time, and if Aunt Jane wondered what was keeping them, she didn't let on, but a smile played over her mouth and she was content inside.

MEDICAL™

Large Print

Titles for the next six months...

December

SINGLE FATHER, WIFE NEEDED	Sarah Morgan
THE ITALIAN DOCTOR'S PERFECT FAMILY	Alison Roberts
A BABY OF THEIR OWN	Gill Sanderson
THE SURGEON AND THE SINGLE MUM	Lucy Clark
HIS VERY SPECIAL NURSE	Margaret McDonagh
THE SURGEON'S LONGED-FOR BRIDE	Emily Forbes

January

SINGLE DAD, OUTBACK WIFE	Amy Andrews
A WEDDING IN THE VILLAGE	Abigail Gordon
IN HIS ANGEL'S ARMS	Lynne Marshall
THE FRENCH DOCTOR'S MIDWIFE BRIDE	Fiona Lowe
A FATHER FOR HER SON	Rebecca Lang
THE SURGEON'S MARRIAGE PROPOSAL	Molly Evans

February

THE ITALIAN GP'S BRIDE	Kate Hardy
THE CONSULTANT'S ITALIAN KNIGHT	Maggie Kingsley
HER MAN OF HONOUR	Melanie Milburne
ONE SPECIAL NIGHT...	Margaret McDonagh
THE DOCTOR'S PREGNANCY SECRET	Leah Martyn
BRIDE FOR A SINGLE DAD	Laura Iding

MILLS & BOON®
Pure reading pleasure

1107 LP 2P P1 Medical

MEDICAL™

Large Print

March

THE SINGLE DAD'S MARRIAGE WISH Carol Marinelli
THE PLAYBOY DOCTOR'S PROPOSAL   Alison Roberts
THE CONSULTANT'S SURPRISE CHILD   Joanna Neil
DR FERRERO'S BABY SECRET   Jennifer Taylor
THEIR VERY SPECIAL CHILD   Dianne Drake
THE SURGEON'S RUNAWAY BRIDE   Olivia Gates

April

THE ITALIAN COUNT'S BABY   Amy Andrews
THE NURSE HE'S BEEN WAITING FOR Meredith Webber
HIS LONG-AWAITED BRIDE   Jessica Matthews
A WOMAN TO BELONG TO   Fiona Lowe
WEDDING AT PELICAN BEACH   Emily Forbes
DR CAMPBELL'S SECRET SON   Anne Fraser

May

THE MAGIC OF CHRISTMAS   Sarah Morgan
THEIR LOST-AND-FOUND FAMILY   Marion Lennox
CHRISTMAS BRIDE-TO-BE   Alison Roberts
HIS CHRISTMAS PROPOSAL   Lucy Clark
BABY: FOUND AT CHRISTMAS   Laura Iding
THE DOCTOR'S PREGNANCY BOMBSHELL Janice Lynn

™ MILLS & BOON®
Pure reading pleasure

1107 LP 2P P2 Medical